Is That a Dead Dog In Your Locker?

D0328364

Is That a Dead Dog In Your Locker?

by Todd Strasser

Scholastic Inc.

New York Toronto London Auckland Sydney
Mexico City New Delhi Hong Kong Buenos Aires

No part of this publication may be reproduced, stored in a retrieval system, or transmitted in any form or by any means, electronic, mechanical, photocopying, recording, or otherwise, without written permission of the publisher. For information regarding permission, write to Scholastic Inc., Attention: Permissions Department, 557 Broadway, New York, NY 10012.

ISBN 0-439-77694-5

Text copyright © 2006 by Todd Strasser.
Cover illustration copyright © 2006 by Greg Swearingen.

All rights reserved. Published by Scholastic Inc.

SCHOLASTIC and associated logos are trademarks and/or registered trademarks of Scholastic Inc.

12 11 10 9 8 7 6 5   7 8 9 10 11/0

Printed in the U.S.A.
First printing, September 2006

To Alex "DDR Pro" Silver
and Abby "Sea Glass" Silver
—TS

Is That a Dead Dog In Your Locker?

AN INTRODUCTION BEGINNING WITH A MESSAGE FROM THE AUTHOR OF THIS BOOK:

Dear Reader,

The words UNDERPANTS and UNDER-WEAR will not appear in this book. Only bad writers with brains the size of cookie crumbs use those words. GREAT AND WISE AUTHORS never stoop to using "bathroom humor," such as SUPER STINKY UNDERPANTS, to make the reader laugh.

The author of this book does not believe in using bathroom humor to get cheap laughs. Therefore, he will use the word UNDERGARMENT, which can be found in the Bible and in the works of the greatest writer ever, William Shakespeare. Like Willy S., the author of this book would HOCK UP A BIG GREEN LOOGIE or ROLL EARWAX INTO TINY LITTLE BALLS before using bathroom humor.

By the way, BIG GREEN LOOGIES and TINY BALLS OF EARWAX come from parts of the body called ORIFICES. Now there's a funny word for you. Here's how you say it: OR-UH-FISS. Go ahead. Give it a try.

The dictionary says an ORIFICE is a mouth-like opening. So if you know someone who talks a lot, you might say that he or she has a big orifice that words come out of. And the next time you get sent to the principal's office, you better make sure you go to the office and not the ORIFICE. Because going to THE PRINCIPAL'S ORIFICE could have very unpleasant results, especially if your principal has BAD BREATH. Even if your principal has A REALLY NICE ORIFICE with a TV or computer, or a fish tank in it. Of course, it would have to be a REALLY BIG ORIFICE to have all that stuff. But as we know, some principals do have REALLY BIG ORIFICES.

And that reminds the author of something else. Some bad writers with brains the size of an amoeba's toenail also try to get cheap laughs by putting phrases like REALLY BIG ORIFICE or SUPER STINKY UNDERPANTS in capital letters. The author of this book thinks that's JUST PLAIN STUPID. He would rather pour a tanker truck worth of mouthwash into a PRINCIPAL'S ORIFICE than try to get a cheap laugh by putting words like ORIFICE in capital letters.

So, to conclude, the author of this book promises that you will not see words like UNDERPANTS or UNDERWEAR in these pages. And if you do see them, the author didn't put them there. Someone else probably snuck into the author's ORIFICE — Oops! I mean, office — and put them in the book when the author wasn't looking. Some really bad writer who probably DOESN'T EVEN WEAR UNDERGARMENTS!

Sincerely,
The Author

THE TOILET TREE MYSTERY

Wade Tardy and his brother Leyton were brothers. Some people called them the Tardy Boys because they were always late. Wade and Leyton had a little brother named TJ. One morning, Wade looked out the kitchen window and saw TJ in the front yard shoveling dirt into a broken toilet.

"What are you doing, TJ?" Wade opened the window and asked.

"Planting a tree," said TJ.

"Why are you planting it in a toilet?" asked Wade.

"Because it has to be a toilet tree," TJ said and dumped another shovelful of dirt into the toilet. Strewn around the Tardy Boys' front yard were broken bicycles, smashed skateboards, bent Razor scooters, partly burned sofas, and broken toilets.

"I've never heard of a toilet tree," said Wade.

"Neither have I," said TJ. "But next summer when I go to sleepaway camp I'm supposed to bring toilet trees."

This sounded strange to Wade, but he had other matters on his mind. "Well, you better finish planting it later," he said. "It's time for breakfast."

Now Leyton Tardy trudged into the kitchen. He and Wade were fraternal twins, which meant they did not look alike. Leyton was tall and handsome with blond hair and broad, muscular shoulders. Wade was thin and scrawny with dark hair. But what Wade lacked in good looks and muscles, he made up for with smarts. If you drilled a tiny orifice into Wade's head and peeked inside, you would find that his skull was stuffed with brain cells.

Leyton slumped into a chair and stared unhappily at the ants crawling around on the kitchen table. Wade could tell something was bothering him. "Is something wrong, Leyton?"

"Yes," answered Leyton. "This afternoon in Ms. Fitt's social studies class I'm supposed to debate against our WORST ARCH-ENEMY EVER. I've already ditched the debate twice and Ms. Fitt says that if I don't debate today I will face THE AWFUL

FATE OF FLUNKDOM and will have to go to summer school."

"Bummer," said Wade.

"Why don't you just do the debate?" asked TJ while he washed the dirt off his hands in the kitchen sink.

"Because I'm not prepared," answered Leyton. If you drilled a tiny orifice into his head and peeked inside, you might see butterflies.

"Why not?" asked TJ.

"Because it's a double period debate and there are way too many topics in Ms. Fitt's debate jar," said Leyton. "The topic could be slavery, or colonialism, or the Constitution. It would take too long to prepare for all that."

"What about your WORST ARCH-ENEMY EVER?" asked TJ. "Do you think he'll be prepared?"

"Yes," said Leyton. "He's an evil nasty mean villainous slimeball with the personality of a toadstool. Nobody wants to hang out with him, so he's probably had days and days to prepare."

"But haven't you also had days and days?" asked TJ.

Wade Tardy and his brother Leyton exchanged a knowing glance. TJ was now nine years old. It was time to explain to him what it meant to be a Tardy Boy.

"Do you know what brainiacs do, TJ?" Wade asked.

"No," said TJ.

"They study hard and get good grades," Wade explained.

"Do you know what jocks do?" Leyton asked.

"Yes!" TJ exclaimed proudly. "They do sports."

"That's right," said Wade. "And do you know what Tardy Boys do?"

TJ shook his head.

"They hang out, and chill, and mostly, they party," said Leyton.

The tiny lines in TJ's forehead creased. "What's that?"

"Well, TJ," said Wade, "to party means to get down and boogie and hang loose and kick back and tear it up."

"That's a lot!" TJ gasped wondrously.

"Yes, it is," said Wade. "And it doesn't leave us time for homework, which is why Leyton is facing THE AWFUL FATE OF FLUNKDOM this afternoon."

Just then the front doorbell rang.

"Go see who it is, Leyton," said Wade.

"Why do I have to go see who it is?" Leyton asked. "Why can't *you* go?"

"Because I'm telling TJ what it means to be a Tardy Boy," said Wade.

"Why can't I tell him?" asked Leyton.

"Go ahead," said Wade, even though he knew Leyton wouldn't be able to.

Leyton tried to think of something to say. The butterflies in his head flapped their wings really hard, but no ideas came. Meanwhile, the doorbell rang again. Leyton left to see who it was. But he wasn't happy.

"Do you never, *ever* do homework?" TJ asked Wade after Leyton left.

"Not if we can avoid it," answered Wade.

"Wow!" said TJ. "When I grow up, can I be a Tardy Boy, too?"

Before Wade could answer, there came an excited shout from the front hall. "Wade! Come quick! It's Daisy and she's in trouble!"

FOUL FRENCH CHEESE DOG BREATH

Wade and TJ rushed to the front door.
Leyton was holding it open and Daisy
Peduncle was standing outside. Daisy's
parents were hippies and Daisy was their
peace-and-love child. Daisy's long, brown
hair was braided and she wore rose-
colored granny glasses. Because she was a
peace-and-love hippie child, she usually

went to school barefoot wearing a long, yellow tie-dyed sundress.

"Hi, Daisy," said Wade. "Leyton said you were in trouble. I hope it's not about the party tonight."

Every Friday after they got home from work, Daisy's parents put on tie-dyed clothes and threw a party. Daisy was allowed to invite all her friends while her parents sat in the living room weaving baskets and listening to peace-and-love music on their iPods.

"The party's not the problem," said Daisy. Then, she pointed to a cardboard box resting on a luggage cart on the front walk. "There's the problem."

"It doesn't look like a problem," said Leyton. "It looks like a box."

"No, duh," said Daisy. "It's not the box

that's the problem. It's what's inside the box." She undid the luggage cart straps and opened the cardboard box. Inside was a model of a building made out of Popsicle sticks, cereal boxes, and toilet paper tubes.

"That's the problem?" asked Leyton.

"No, that's a model of the state capitol I made for the architectural competition today," Daisy said, and carefully lifted the roof off the model. Inside was a brown ball of fur that smelled awful. The Tardy Boys pinched their noses and stepped back.

"Why is there a brown ball of fur in your model of the state capitol?" Wade asked.

"And why does it smell so gross?" asked Leyton.

"It's not a brown ball of fur," replied Daisy. "It's Mr. Roy's old pug dog, Wheezy. And that smell is foul French cheese dog breath."

"If he's a pug dog, why doesn't he have a head and tail and legs?" asked TJ.

"And why does he have such awful breath?" asked Leyton.

"He does have a head, tail, and legs," answered Daisy. "But when he sleeps he likes to tuck his head and legs and tail into a ball. And the reason his breath is so awful is because Mr. Roy feeds him French cheese."

Daisy opened her backpack, took out a plastic container, and pried open the lid. Inside was a round white disk of soft cheese that smelled so bad it made your nose want to jump off your face and run away. The Tardy Boys squeezed their noses even tighter and stepped back even farther. By now they were practically in the street.

"Put the lid back on!" TJ cried.

"That smells even worse than Wheezy's breath," gasped Leyton.

"Why can't Mr. Roy feed Wheezy normal dog food?" Wade asked.

"I don't know," said Daisy. "I usually just take Wheezy for walks in the afternoon while Mr. Roy is at work. But this morning Mr. Roy had an emergency and he was in a really big rush. He rang my doorbell and asked me to take Wheezy all day. He told me to give Wheezy a wedge of cheese and started to say something about some pills, but then he left so fast I didn't hear it all."

Daisy reached down into the model of the state capitol and gently patted the sleeping ball of stinky fur.

"How can you stand that smell, Daisy?" Leyton asked.

"I'm not sure," Daisy answered. "But I think it's because I'm a peace-and-love hippie child and to hippie children all the world smells sweet."

"Right now the world smells like foul French cheese dog breath," Wade said. "So could you do us a favor and put the roof back on your model?"

Daisy put the roof on, once again covering Wheezy and his awful smell. The Tardy Boys stepped closer.

"Why couldn't you leave Wheezy home for the day?" Wade asked.

"Because someone has to walk him and give him his cheese," Daisy said. "Wheezy's an old dog and he has to be walked every hour and a half or he does his business in the house."

"Wheezy's in business?" TJ asked.

"No, TJ," said Wade. "Doing his business is another way of saying he'd go to the bathroom in the house."

"But most of us go to the bathroom in the house," said TJ.

"Yes, but when Wheezy does it, he doesn't actually use the bathroom," Wade tried to explain.

"And my parents don't want dogs doing their business in the house," Daisy said and looked at her watch. "It's late and I have to get to school. I was hoping I could leave Wheezy here and one of you would ditch school and take care of him for me."

Wade and Leyton shared a pensive glance. Daisy was their good friend, and her parents threw the most awesome parties, so they wanted to help her.

"You know, Daisy, we would do anything for you," Wade said. "But I don't think either Leyton or TJ or I can stay home and take care of Wheezy today."

Daisy's shoulders slumped with disappointment. "Then what will I do?"

"Take Wheezy to school with you," said TJ.

"I can't," said Daisy. "It violates the NFA rule."

The NFA (No Furry Animals) rule was established the day Fibby (short for Fibula) Mandible began to go to The School With No Name. Fibby Mandible was allergic to animal fur. She was not allergic to milk, nuts, chocolate, vegetables, berries, dust, pollen, smoke, math, or gym, even though her mother said she was.

"Rules are meant to be broken," Wade declared.

"But what if Assistant Principal Snout sees Wheezy?" Daisy asked. Assistant

Principal Snout lived in fear of students, germs, and Ulna Mandible, the mother of Fibby Mandible.

Wade thought about what might happen if Assistant Principal Snout found Wheezy in The School With No Name. Then he had an idea. "Could you hide Wheezy in your locker?"

"I guess," said Daisy. "As long as he gets to eat French cheese and has a walk every hour and a half."

Wade turned to his brother. "I think we should try to help Daisy. Even if our noses never forgive us."

"Oh, thank you!" Daisy cried. "You're the best friends a hippie peace-and-love child could have."

The Tardy Boys told Daisy to wait while they finished getting ready for school. On the way back inside, TJ, Leyton, and Wade passed the broken bicycles, smashed skateboards, and bent Razor scooters scattered around the front lawn. They stopped beside the broken toilet TJ had filled with dirt.

"Maybe a toilet tree isn't a tree that grows in a toilet," said Leyton. "Maybe it's a tree that grows toilets."

"How?" Wade asked.

"Like apples grow on apple trees," Leyton explained. "Maybe toilets grow on toilet trees."

"Leyton, that has to be the dumbest thing you've ever said," snorted Wade. "Next, you'll be telling us that there are shoe trees and family trees."

Wade and TJ laughed and headed inside. Leyton followed, narrowing his eyes angrily at his brother. He was getting tired of Wade always telling him how dumb he was.

THE TERRIBLE STENCH OF TOE CHEESE

Later, the Tardy Boys and Daisy walked to school. Daisy pulled the cart with the cardboard box strapped to it. They could hear the old pug wheezing peacefully inside. On the sidewalk they suddenly encountered another awful stink in the air. But unlike the rich, pungent odor of foul French cheese dog breath, this new smell was sharp and bitter and burned the inside of your nose.

TJ wrinkled his nose. "What's that new terrible smell?"

"It smells like feet that haven't been washed for years," said Leyton, pinching his nose.

A moment later they passed a yard with a small, black dog on a short leash. The little dog was pulling against the leash and whimpering sadly as if it wished it could get free and run around.

Then they passed another yard with a large brown dog who kept scratching its ear as if it would not stop itching.

Meanwhile the terrible unwashed foot odor hung in the air.

Next they passed a yard in which an overweight white dog lay on its side panting as if it was too tired to get up.

And the terrible stench of unwashed feet smelled even stronger!

Suddenly Leyton exclaimed excitedly, "I know what it is!"

Wade, Daisy, and TJ stopped. It was rare that Leyton actually had an idea, and they were eager to hear it.

"Those sad-looking dogs and that new terrible smell," Leyton said. "It must be a WHOLE series of unfortunate smelly dogs!"

Wade listened in stunned silence. Sometimes he worried that his twin brother suffered from a dislocated brain.

"It's not those other dogs," someone said.

The Tardy Boys and Daisy turned. Coming toward them was their friend Al-Ian Konspiracy. Al-Ian was a friendly boy and a brainiac who believed in aliens and UFOs.

"Then what's making that smell?" asked Daisy.

Al-Ian pointed at the sidewalk where a clear trail of slime glimmered in the morning sunlight. "What you smell is toe cheese. And it was left by the same person who left this trail of slime."

The Tardy Boys shared a grim look. Only one person was capable of leaving a trail of slime.

"What is toe cheese?" asked TJ.

"I'll tell you," Al-Ian said. "But first let's cross to the other side of the street where the smell isn't so bad."

They crossed the street, then continued toward The School With No Name.

"Toe cheese is the mushy, smelly stuff between your toes and under your toe nails," Al-Ian explained.

"Is toe cheese made from the same things as other cheese?" asked TJ.

"No," answered Al-Ian. "The main ingredient of regular cheese is milk. The main ingredient of toe cheese is dead skin. Mixed into it are sock fibers, which give toe cheese colors such as white, gray, or red. Then there's sweat, which gives it that moist, mushy quality. And bacteria, which gives it that foul fragrance. And the final ingredient is fungus, which, like the French, love to eat smelly cheese."

"If the French like smelly cheese, do they eat toe cheese?" asked TJ.

"The only French people who eat toe cheese are those who can eat potato chips with their toes," answered Al-Ian.

The Tardy Boys would have asked more questions, but they'd arrived at The School With No Name where a loud argument was under way.

THE SHRIEK OF ULNA MANDIBLE

Standing in front of The School With No Name was a tall man with gray hair. He wore a dark blue suit. His name was Mr. Stratemeyer and he was NOT the Tardy Boys' worst arch-enemy ever. He was the principal of The School With No Name and the boss of Assistant Principal Snout.

Assistant Principal Snout was also NOT the Tardy Boys' worst arch-enemy ever.

Assistant Principal Snout wore dark slacks and a white shirt and red tie. He also wore a white breathing mask over his mouth and nose, bright yellow foam earplugs in his ears, and light blue latex gloves. He wore the mask and gloves because he was terrified of germs and knew that middle school students were full of them. He wore the earplugs because he lived in fear of THE SHRIEK OF ULNA MANDIBLE.

Principal Stratemeyer and Assistant Principal Snout were listening while Ulna Mandible yelled at them. Ulna Mandible was NOT the Tardy Boys' worst arch-enemy ever, although she came pretty close. Ulna Mandible was Fibby Mandible's mother, and she was not to be messed with if you valued your life. Ulna Mandible knew of only five ways to speak:

shouting, yelling, screaming, screeching, and shrieking.

Standing behind Ulna was Fibby Mandible herself. Fibby Mandible was NOT the Tardy Boys' worst arch-enemy ever, although she came even closer than her mom. Fibby had streaked blond hair and a freckled nose. She liked to stand behind her mother with her arms crossed and a smug smile on her face whenever Ulna screamed at people. That meant Fibby spent A LOT OF TIME standing behind her mother.

"You know quite well that my daughter is not only afraid of dogs, but allergic to their fur!" Ulna shouted at Principal Stratemeyer and Assistant Principal Snout. *"And yet everyday you let people bring their dogs onto school property!"*

"Is that true?" Principal Stratemeyer asked Assistant Principal Snout.

"Not exactly," answered Assistant Principal Snout. "Some parents drive their children to school in their cars. And sometimes they also have their dogs in their cars. But the dogs always stay in the cars."

"That's not good enough!" Ulna Mandible shrieked.

"Mrs. Mandible," Principal Stratemeyer said. "We can't stop people from taking their dogs in their cars when they drive their children to school."

"The NFA rule clearly states that no furry animals are allowed on school property," Ulna yelled.

The only reason The School With No Name even had the NFA rule was because

Fibby's mother had hired the law firm of Lamb, Shank, and Loin to go to court to get it.

"*I'll take you to court!*" Ulna screamed. "*I'll sue!*"

While Ulna shouted at the principals, Fibby noticed the Tardy Boys and Daisy and Al-Ian. Fibby Mandible didn't like the Tardy Boys because Wade and Leyton were popular and liked to have fun and were happy even though they didn't have a mother who screamed at school principals for them.

Fibby Mandible didn't like Daisy because Daisy came to school barefoot each day in a baggy yellow tie-dyed sundress and wore ugly glasses even though she was beautiful. Even worse, Daisy was popular and her parents threw great parties.

It didn't matter whether or not Fibby liked TJ Tardy because he'd already left for the elementary school.

When Assistant Principal Snout saw the Tardy Boys, he checked his watch. *Late as usual*, he thought. When Fibby saw the box on Daisy's luggage cart, she left her mother and came over. Even though Fibby didn't like Daisy, she was *dying* to see what Daisy had made for the architectural competition.

"Hi, Daisy," Fibby said. "Can I see your model?"

Daisy undid the straps and opened the box.

Fibby snickered. "Oh, how cute! The state capitol building made out of Popsicle sticks and cereal boxes and toilet paper tubes. You don't really think that's going to win the competition, do you?"

"Well, where's your entry?" Daisy asked.

Fibby pointed at the curb where her mother's bright red Hummer was parked. On a trailer behind the Hummer was a perfect scale model of the White House made out of thousands of small sugar cubes held together with Elmer's glue. It was nearly six feet wide and four feet tall.

"Wow, that's awesome, Fibby," said Wade. "Your mom did a really great job building it for you."

Fibby put her hands on her hips and stuck her freckled nose into the air. "For your information, my mom didn't build it."

This was true. Even Ulna Mandible couldn't have created such a perfect model of the White House. Instead, she hired a professional model builder to do the job for her.

As Fibby stood near Daisy's model of the

state capitol building, her nose began to itch. Her eyes began to water. "Achoo!" she sneezed.

Ulna Mandible heard the sneeze and rushed to her daughter's side. *"Fibula, my darling!"* she screamed. *"What's wrong?!"*

WADE'S WHEEZING STOMACH

"Achoo!" Fibby Mandible sneezed again. Ulna Mandible quickly opened the black medical bag she always carried. Other mothers carried shoulder bags or handbags, but Ulna preferred the medical bag so that she could have instant access to all the medicines her daughter might require. She took out a tissue and wiped her

daughter's nose. Then she gave Fibby
an inhaler to breathe through while
she took her temperature with an ear
thermometer. All the while she shrieked,
*"Call the police! Call emergency services!
My daughter is having a severe allergic
reaction!"*

"All she did was sneeze," said Principal
Stratemeyer.

*"If you don't call the police right now, I'll
sue!"* Ulna Mandible screamed.

"Why don't we wait a minute and see,"
suggested Principal Stratemeyer.

*"One minute could be the difference between
life and death!"* Ulna Mandible yelled.

"Your daughter doesn't look like she's
dying," said Principal Stratemeyer.

Using a digital blood pressure monitor,
Ulna took Fibby's pulse and blood

pressure. Everything was normal. It looked like Fibby would live.

Suddenly, a wheezing sound came from the model of the state capitol building inside the box on Daisy's luggage cart.

"*What was that?!*" shouted Ulna Mandible.

Wade Tardy knew that Wheezy had made the sound. He also knew that if Ulna Mandible discovered Wheezy on school property, she would sue the school and the town and the world. And if there were any aliens around, she would probably sue them, too.

Wade stepped next to the cardboard box and said, "It's my stomach. I guess I'm hungry."

"When people are hungry their stomachs don't wheeze," Fibby said. "Their stomachs growl."

"Actually, it depends on *how* hungry I am," said Wade. "If I'm just a little hungry, my stomach wheezes. If I'm more hungry than that, it growls."

Woof! From inside the box came a bark. Sometimes, when Wheezy was in the middle of a dream that involved other dogs, he barked in his sleep.

"*What was THAT?!*" shrieked Ulna Mandible.

Thinking fast, Wade cried, "Oh, my gosh! We're late for school!" Daisy grabbed the handle of the luggage cart and, along with the Tardy Boys and Al-Ian, hurried past the principals and Ulna and Fibby Mandible.

"Stop!" Assistant Principal Snout shouted. "Hold it right there!" He followed the Tardy Boys and their friends into the school lobby, leaving Principal Stratemeyer to deal with THE SHRIEK OF ULNA MANDIBLE.

"Hold what right where?" Leyton asked.

"Hold it, right here!" Assistant Principal Snout pointed at the lobby floor.

The Tardy Boys and their friends looked down.

"Hold what?" asked Al-Ian.

"It," said Assistant Principal Snout.

"But we don't know what it is," said Daisy.

"Yes!" Assistant Principal Snout said. "That's it!"

"What's it?" asked Leyton.

Assistant Principal Snout squinted his eyes and grit his teeth. "It . . . is the reason I want all of you in my office. Now!"

THE LINE THAT COULD NOT BE CROSSED

Assistant Principal Snout marched them toward his office. Normally, going to the principal's office did not bother the Tardy Boys, but today was different. If Assistant Principal Snout discovered that Wheezy was in Daisy's model of the state capitol, it would mean serious trouble.

They stopped at the sink outside Assistant Principal Snout's door.

"You know what to do," said the assistant principal.

No one was allowed to enter Assistant Principal Snout's office without first washing his or her hands. Next they had to leave their shoes on the mat outside the door.

Inside the office, a large hypoallergenic air purifier hummed. Assistant Principal Snout sat down at his desk. On the shelf behind him were three large boxes. One contained white breathing masks. Another contained light blue latex gloves. The third contained bright yellow foam earplugs.

Four chairs lined the wall as far from the assistant principal's desk as possible. On the floor between the chairs and the desk was a painted red line. A sign next to the red line read:

STUDENTS DO NOT

CROSS THIS LINE

Seated at his desk, Assistant Principal Snout removed the bright yellow earplugs from his ears and dropped them into the wastepaper can. Now that he was safe in his office, he did not have to fear THE SHRIEK OF ULNA MANDIBLE. He also took off his breathing mask. Now that he was in the same room with the hypoallergenic air purifier, he did not have to worry about breathing the same air students breathed. Next he took off his blue latex gloves. Now that he was on the other side of the red line, he did not have to worry about being touched by germ-ridden students.

The Tardy Boys and their friends sat in the chairs on the other side of the office. Daisy parked the luggage cart beside her chair and prayed that Wheezy would not wheeze or snort or bark.

"Do you know why I told you to come to my office?" Assistant Principal Snout asked from behind his desk.

"Because you needed an excuse to get away from THE SHRIEK OF ULNA MANDIBLE," said Al-Ian.

Assistant Principal Snout blinked and cleared his throat. "True, but I meant, the *other* reason why I told you to come to my office."

The Tardy Boys and their friends shook their heads.

"It's because you're always late for school," said the assistant principal as he picked up the phone. "And I've decided it's time to speak to your parents about that."

"But we haven't seen our parents in years," said Leyton.

"We don't even know where they are," added Wade.

"How can that be?" Assistant Principal Snout asked.

"We don't know," said Wade. "They went away a long time ago and we haven't heard from them since."

"Maybe they're being held by an evil villain," Daisy said. "Or maybe they died in a terrible fire. That's what usually happens in kids' books."

"But this isn't a kids' book," said Assistant Principal Snout. "This is real life and I need someone to call."

40

"You can call my parents," said Al-Ian. "If they haven't been kidnapped by aliens."

"Good." Assistant Principal Snout began to dial. Suddenly there was loud, rapid knocking on the office door, and Olga Shotput, the school's silver medalist janitor, rushed in. Olga was a large woman with short hair and muscular arms who had come to the United States many years ago to compete in the Spring Olympics. Her face was red and she was breathing hard.

"Is something wrong?" asked Assistant Principal Snout.

Olga clicked her heels together and saluted. "Assistant Principal Snout, sir, I believe I have earned a gold medal in custodianship!"

Assistant Principal Snout let out a deep, sad sigh. He had heard this request many times before. "Olga, you are a wonderful janitor. And if there were such a thing as a gold medal in custodianship, I would give it to you. But there's no such thing."

Olga's shoulders sagged and she gazed down sadly at the silver medal that hung from her neck on a red, white, and blue ribbon. Only it wasn't really a medal, it was the top from a can of tuna fish. Her eyes began to water.

"Please don't cry, Olga," said Assistant Principal Snout. "Think of how few people in the world have won even a silver medal. You should be proud."

"Proud of what?" Olga sniffed. "If you win a silver medal, the only thing it qualifies you for is a career as a janitor!" She burst into tears.

Assistant Principal Snout turned to the Tardy Boys and their friends. "Go to class. I'll talk to you later."

The Tardy Boys, Daisy, and Al-Ian left Assistant Principal Snout with Olga, the sobbing silver-medalist janitor. When they got to Daisy's locker, the boys stood close and blocked the view while Daisy gently lifted Wheezy out of the model of the state capitol building and placed him comfortably in her locker.

When Al-Ian saw Wheezy, his eyes went wide. "Why are you putting that smelly old pug dog in your locker?"

"Shhh!" Wade pressed a finger to his lips. With his other hand he held his nose and tried not to inhale Wheezy's foul French cheese dog breath.

Daisy quietly closed the locker door. "We have to take care of him today," she whispered.

"But what about the NFA rule?" Al-Ian asked.

"He'll sleep all day," Daisy said. "All we have to do is feed him French cheese and make sure he does his business. Then at the end of the day we can take him home and go back to my house and have a party."

"Did you say party?" someone behind them asked.

The Tardy Boys and their friends spun around. Standing behind them was Ms. Fitt, their social studies teacher!

THE ODOR OF CAMEMBERT

Ms. Fitt had red hair that hung down past her shoulders in ringlets. She liked to wear big earrings and colorful clothes. Today, she was wearing a bright yellow turtleneck sweater, an orange felt skirt, and green-and-white cowboy boots. Ms. Fitt was everybody's favorite teacher because she liked kids and made learning interesting.

When she got close to Daisy's locker, Ms. Fitt wrinkled her nose. "Is that Camembert?"

"No, it's barf green," said Leyton, thinking that she was asking about the color of the locker.

"No, I meant the smell," said Ms. Fitt. "Camembert is the smelliest of all the smelly French cheeses. I guess someone's having it for lunch. Anyway, did I hear you say something about a party?"

"My parents are having one tonight," said Daisy.

"I hope I'll be celebrating, too," said Ms. Fitt. "Today's my annual review. Principal Stratemeyer and some members of the school board are coming to my class to make sure I'm doing a good job as a teacher."

"If you want to look like you're doing a

good job, you should let me ditch the debate today," Leyton said.

Ms. Fitt gave Leyton a sympathetic look. "I'm sorry, Leyton, but I can't. Being a good teacher means treating all students equally. Every student has to participate in the debate. It wouldn't be fair to the others if I let you ditch again. You understand, don't you?"

Leyton sighed and nodded. Ms. Fitt was a good and fair teacher and wouldn't make him face THE AWFUL FATE OF FLUNKDOM unless she absolutely had to. She patted him on the shoulder. "Don't ditch the debate today, Leyton. Come to class and give it your best shot. We'll all be rooting for you." She left and went down the hall.

"Guess we better get to class," said Wade.

Daisy looked at her watch. "Oh, no! It's

already been an hour since Wheezy last ate French cheese and did his business. I don't know if he can hold it until the end of next period."

"Let's keep our fingers crossed," said Wade. "Can we all meet back here as soon as the period ends?"

"Yes," said Daisy and Leyton.

"If I haven't been kidnapped by aliens," said Al-Ian.

THE ALIENS FROM THE PLANET CHEESE

As Al-Ian walked down the hall, a metallic clinking sound came from under his shirt.

"What's that sound, Al-Ian?" Leyton asked.

Al-Ian pulled out a chain with two small flat pieces of metal. "Intergalactic Return Address Dog Tags," he said. "They have my name and address, as well as the location of Planet Earth in the Milky Way

Galaxy, so that the aliens will know where to return my body once they have finished experimenting with it."

"Couldn't you just tell them where you live?" Daisy asked.

"They might not understand English," Al-Ian said. "They might not even have ears. That's why the Intergalactic Return Address Dog Tags have diagrams showing where Earth is."

"What if the aliens don't have eyes?" Leyton asked.

"That's ridiculous, Leyton." Wade chuckled. "If they didn't have eyes, how could they find their way around the universe?"

Leyton balled his hands into angry fists. He hated when his brother made fun of him. "Maybe they *smell* their way around the universe, okay?"

Wade thought his brother's idea was so dumb it was funny. "Right! Then you won't have to worry about being kidnapped, Al-Ian. One whiff of Wheezy's foul French cheese dog breath and those aliens will blast off toward the next galaxy as fast as they can."

Wade and Al-Ian laughed. But Leyton didn't. He was still angry at his brother. A few moments later they all got to their classes. As the period passed Daisy wondered if Wheezy could hold it until she returned. Wade wondered if TJ could really grow a tree in the broken toilet in the front yard. Leyton wondered if he would ever have a good idea. Al-Ian wondered what alien kidnappers would find if they decided to drill a tiny orifice into his skull and look inside.

As soon as the period ended they all jumped up from their desks. As Wade rushed down the hall toward Daisy's locker he noticed an unpleasant odor in the air. Kids in the hallway were holding their noses and fanning their faces.

"You think it's Wheezy?" Leyton whispered when he came out of his classroom and joined his brother in the hall.

"I'm not sure," said Wade, noticing a trail of clear slime on the hallway floor.

As they got closer to Daisy's locker, the smell got stronger. Daisy and Al-Ian joined them.

"I have a bad feeling about this," Wade said nervously.

"It could be aliens," said Al-Ian.

"If it is, they must be really smelly aliens," said Leyton.

"Maybe they're THE STINKY ALIENS FROM PLANET CHEESE!" gasped Al-Ian.

"Achoo!" Someone sneezed behind them. The Tardy Boys, Daisy, and Al-Ian spun around. It was Fibby Mandible.

"Achoo!" Fibby sneezed again and blew her nose into a tissue. "There must be something nearby that I'm allergic to."

The Tardy Boys and their friends shared nervous looks.

"Maybe it's the awful smell," said Al-Ian.

"No, I'm not allergic to smells," said Fibby. "Even smells as bad as this. I know I'm allergic to animal fur, and my mother says I'm also allergic to milk, nuts, chocolate, vegetables, berries, dust, pollen, smoke, math, and gym. Achoo!"

Fibby opened her backpack and dug around inside until she found her inhaler. She pressed it to her lips and breathed in. Her face turned pink. She breathed in again. Her face turned red.

"*It's not working!*" she screeched. "*Help!*"

The sound of a student crying *help!* in the middle of the hall brought teachers running from all directions. In the confusion that followed, Daisy was able to sneak Wheezy into the cardboard box.

Meanwhile, red-faced Fibby collapsed into the arms of a teacher who helped her lie on her back in the hall. Ms. Fitt took off her bright yellow sweater and balled it into a pillow for Fibby's head. Fibby lay on the hallway floor with her eyes closed. Her skin turned ghostly pale.

"What should we do?" asked Ms. Fitt.

Without opening her eyes, Fibby took a cell phone from her pocket. "Call my mother."

"I don't know her number," said Ms. Fitt.

Even though she appeared to be unconscious, Fibby told her which button to hit for speed dial. In the meantime, Wade motioned to Leyton to pick up the cardboard box with Wheezy inside.

"Why can't you pick it up for once?" Leyton hissed.

"Just do it," Wade hissed back.

Leyton hated the way his brother bossed him around. He picked up the box, but it slid in his hands.

"Arf!" Inside the box, Wheezy barked when he was suddenly jostled.

Even though she was near death, Fibby Mandible suddenly sat up and opened her eyes. "What was that?!" she demanded.

WADE'S BARKING STOMACH

With the box still in his hands, Leyton froze.

"Well? What was it?" Fibby crossed her arms and looked very much alive.

"It, uh, was my stomach," Wade said.

"I thought your stomach wheezes and growls," said Fibby. "Since when does it bark?"

"When I'm a little hungry it wheezes," Wade said. "When I'm just regular hungry it growls. But when I'm *really* hungry it barks."

Fibby frowned, but then someone said, "Ms. Take is coming!"

Ms. Take was the school nurse. Fibby spent more time in the nurse's office than in any other room in the school. When she heard that Ms. Take was coming, Fibby forgot about Wade's barking stomach and lay down. She closed her eyes and once again looked very pale.

It was time to take Wheezy outside. Daisy nodded at Wade and Leyton, who carried the cardboard box down to the end of the hall and turned left. Halfway down the next hallway they came to **THE SECRET DOOR TO THE OUTSIDE**.

Leyton knew it was **THE SECRET DOOR TO THE OUTSIDE** because **THE SECRET DOOR TO THE OUTSIDE** was printed on it in big black letters.

"How can it be a secret if **THE SECRET DOOR TO THE OUTSIDE** is painted on it?" asked Wade.

"Maybe it's **THE SECRET DOOR TO THE OUTSIDE** because it's invisible and we're the only ones who can see it!" said Leyton, thinking he'd finally had a good idea.

"Don't be ridiculous, Leyton," Wade said. "*Everyone* can see it."

Leyton grit his teeth. If Wade didn't stop making fun of him, there was going to be serious trouble. Just then, Al-Ian came down the hall.

"Al-Ian, stop," said Leyton. He pointed at the door. "Do you see **THE SECRET DOOR TO THE OUTSIDE**?"

Al-Ian shook his head.

"You see?!" Leyton turned to his brother. "You think you're so smart, but it is an INVISIBLE **SECRET DOOR TO THE OUTSIDE** that only the Tardy Boys can see!"

"Ha! Ha!" Al-Ian started to laugh.

Leyton frowned. "Why are you laughing?"

"You believed me," said Al-Ian. "**THE SECRET DOOR TO THE OUTSIDE** isn't invisible. I can see it with my own eyes."

Leyton's face turned red with embarrassment. Once again they were laughing at him. He took a marker out of his pocket and added the words *not so* to the door. Then he pushed it open. Daisy followed while Wade wedged a piece of paper in the doorway so that the door wouldn't lock behind them.

Al-Ian followed them to the doorway, but went no further.

"Aren't you coming, Al-Ian?" Wade asked.

Al-Ian stuck his head outside and peered up at the sky. "I don't think so," he said, and backed away from the door.

Outside, Daisy and Wade waited while Leyton opened the box, then staggered back and clapped his hand over his mouth and nose. "Gross!"

Wade didn't have to ask what his brother was talking about. Now that the box was open, the most terrible rich pungent odor rose out of it.

"He's just a little old dog," Daisy said with a sniff.

"No, he's not," said Leyton. "He's a four-legged foul French cheese dog breath machine. How can such a little old dog smell so bad?"

Daisy's eyes began to fill with tears. "It's not his fault." She reached into the box and gently lifted Wheezy out. The little dog's eyes were still closed.

"Don't you have to wake him up?" Leyton asked.

"No," said Daisy. "Wheezy can do his business in his sleep. His old legs are so stiff that he can stand up and not even know it."

"That's right!" Leyton cried excitedly. "I've read that cows can also sleep standing up. Haven't you ever heard of cow tipping?!"

BUSTED!!!!

"What is cow tipping?" Daisy asked.

"It's when people sneak up on sleeping cows and push them over," Wade said. "But it's not true. Cows don't really sleep standing up."

"Yes, they do!" Leyton insisted.

"I hope it's not true. It sounds mean," said Daisy while she gently arranged Wheezy's stiff old legs on the grass so that he was standing in his sleep. Then she kneeled on the ground beside him and whispered in his ear.

The Tardy Boys watched in amazement while Wheezy, with his eyes still closed, slowly lifted his back leg and did his business. When he was finished his leg came back down. All the while the old dog wheezed steadily as if in a deep sleep.

"What did you whisper in his ear?" Wade asked.

"Mr. Roy told me to whisper, 'Wheezy, go,'" answered Daisy.

"I think it's time for us to go, too," Leyton said.

Daisy and Wade gave him strange looks.

"I meant, go back into school," Leyton explained.

"Okay," Daisy said. "Just let me give Wheezy his cheese." She opened the plastic container and took out a wedge of French cheese. Along with the wedge came the rich and pungent odor of Camembert.

"Gross!" Leyton exclaimed as he and Wade backed away, pinching their noses to keep them from jumping off their faces and running away.

Daisy held the wedge of cheese close to Wheezy's face. With the odor of cheese in his little pug nose, the old dog suddenly opened his eyes and ate the wedge from her hand. Then his eyes closed and his head drooped.

Meanwhile, Wade looked in the cardboard box. Lots of loose brown fur lay on the bottom. "Wheezy sure does shed a lot."

"That's strange," said Daisy. "I don't remember Mr. Roy saying anything about him shedding." She placed Wheezy in the box. The little dog rolled into a headless, tailless, legless ball, and went back to sleep. "Let's go inside. We'll meet at my locker after two more periods to sneak Wheezy out again."

"You carry the box, Leyton," Wade said. "I'll get the door."

But Leyton was tired of being bossed around. "How about you get the box and I get the door?"

"Why?" Wade asked.

"Because the box stinks," said Leyton.

"Now that it's been opened, it shouldn't be that bad," said Wade.

Leyton bent over the box and took a sniff. "You're wrong, Wade. It still smells terrible."

"Look, Leyton, we don't have time to argue about this," said Wade. "We're going to be late for our next class."

But Leyton still refused to pick up the box. "Who made you the boss? I'm tired of you acting like I can't think for myself."

Now Wade was starting to get annoyed. "You're the one who got the good looks and the big muscles, okay? You think it would be fair if you were really good-looking and had muscles, *and* had a brain?"

Leyton got a pained look on his handsome face. "But I do have a brain."

"Of course, you do," Daisy said gently. "It's just . . . well, a *different* sort of brain."

"I still don't see why I have to take orders from you," Leyton said to Wade.

"Okay, okay! I'll carry the box," grumbled Wade. "You open the door."

"I can't," said Leyton.

"Why not?" asked Daisy.

"Because we're already outside," said Leyton.

"So?" said Wade.

"So if we go through **THE** *not so* **SECRET DOOR TO THE OUTSIDE** again, we'll be *even farther* outside."

Wade stared at his brother in wonder. Sometimes the kid acted so clueless he'd need a recipe to make ice cubes.

"No, Leyton, look." Daisy pointed at the door. Since they were *already* outside, the writing on the door said **THE SECRET DOOR TO THE INSIDE**.

"Oh, okay." Leyton sighed with relief and reached for the door, then suddenly stopped and cried, "Oh, no! We're busted!!!!"

THE WORLD'S BIGGEST SLIMEBALL

Standing in the doorway was Barton Slugg. Fibby Mandible may not have liked the Tardy Boys, but it was Barton Slugg who really hated them. Barton had buckteeth and brown hair that fell into his beady little eyes. He was the meanest kid in school and the Tardy Boys' WORST ARCH-ENEMY EVER! If the Tardy Boys had been sleeping cows, Barton Slugg would have tipped them over. If Barton Slugg had been an alien kidnapper, he would have left Al-Ian on Uranus instead of returning him to Earth. Barton Slugg had the personality of a toadstool, and left a trail of slime wherever he went.

The smell of Barton Slugg's toe cheese was sharp and bitter and burned the inside of your nose. It was SO bad it formed a cloud around Barton's feet.

"What's in the box?" Barton asked as the odor of toe cheese filled the air and made everyone's nose want to jump off their faces and run away.

"Nothing," said Leyton.

"Looks kind of heavy for nothing," said Barton.

"It's none of your business," said Daisy.

Barton crossed his arms. As long as he blocked the doorway, Daisy and the Tardy Boys could not get back into school.

"Get out of the way," Wade said.

"Not until you tell me what's in that box," said Barton.

Daisy, Leyton, and Wade turned away and spoke in low voices so that Barton couldn't hear them.

"We're in a tough spot," Wade whispered. "What should we do?"

"I could punch him in the nose," whispered Leyton.

"No!" protested Daisy. "Peace-and-love hippie children don't believe in punching anyone in the nose."

"And punching kids' noses usually involves a lot of yelling and crying," added Wade. "Which is sure to bring Assistant Principal Snout running."

"And if Assistant Principal Snout comes, he might see Wheezy," added Daisy.

"Then how will we get back inside?" asked Leyton.

"Hey, guys, what's up?" Al-Ian was standing behind Barton Slugg in the doorway. On his head was something black that looked like a bonnet.

"What's on your head, Al-Ian?" Leyton asked.

"A Velostat Thought-Screen Helmet," Al-Ian explained. "It stops aliens from reading my mind and controlling my thoughts. If they can't control my thoughts, it makes it harder to kidnap me. Except for the Hypno Aliens from the Planet Hocus in the Pocus Galaxy who use direct-hypnotic staring to gain control of their victims."

Barton Slugg turned from the doorway

and glared at Al-Ian. "You're a total nut job."

That was just what the Tardy Boys needed. When Barton Slugg turned from the doorway, Wade picked up Wheezy's box and slipped inside. Daisy and Leyton quickly followed.

"Darn it!" Barton snarled.

The Tardy Boys, Daisy, and Al-Ian hurried down the hall toward Daisy's locker. Al-Ian's Velostat Thought-Screen Helmet covered most of his head. His Intergalactic Return Address Dog Tags jingled under his shirt. "Why did Barton Slugg call me a total nut job?" he asked.

"I can't imagine why," answered Daisy.

"Do you think he's jealous because he's not invited to the party tonight?" Al-Ian asked.

"That must be it," said Daisy. By now

they'd gotten to her locker. The boys stood around in a circle and shielded Daisy while she quickly transferred Wheezy from the box to the locker.

"Aha!" someone said. "Now I know what you're up to!"

The boys and Daisy spun around to find Barton Slugg. From the trail of slime on the hallway floor they realized that he had followed them.

"You're hiding a dog in your locker," Barton exclaimed.

"Keep it down!" Wade said.

"And you're having a party tonight and I'm not invited," said Barton.

"So? We *never* invite you to our parties," said Leyton.

Barton pointed at Al-Ian. "How can you invite a total nut job like him and not invite me?"

"Because he's nice and you're mean," said Daisy.

Barton narrowed his eyes menacingly. "Either invite me to your party or I'll tell Assistant Principal Snout what's in your locker."

"You wouldn't dare," said Leyton.

"Oh, yeah?" said Barton.

Just then Assistant Principal Snout came around the corner wearing his white breathing mask, bright yellow earplugs, and blue latex gloves.

"Assistant Principal Snout!" Barton waved. "Come see what's in Daisy's locker!"

FURRY UNDERGARMENTS

Assistant Principal Snout didn't want to look inside Daisy's locker. Student lockers were filled with germs and other terrible things, including sock fibers, dead skin, fungus, and bacteria. The only reason the contents of student lockers didn't turn into toe cheese was the absence of sweat. This, however, is why the contents of student gym lockers often do turn into toe cheese.

"Why do you want me to look in Daisy's locker?" Assistant Principal Snout asked, nervously adjusting the white breathing mask that covered his nose and mouth.

"Because there's something in there that I think you'll want to see," said Barton Slugg.

"I strongly doubt there's anything in there that I'd *want* to see," replied Assistant Principal Snout as he pulled his blue latex gloves on tighter.

"But it's something that breaks the NFA rule," said Barton Slugg.

Assistant Principal Snout didn't like to hear that there was anything in school that might break the NFA rule. Assistant Principal Snout himself had nothing against furry creatures except that *they did not wear UNDERGARMENTS.**

    * Actually, it is quite possible that some furry creatures DO wear UNDERGARMENTS.

        1. But if they do, those UNDERGARMENTS are probably made of fur.

            a. Thus it is very hard to tell if a furry creature is wearing FURRY UNDERGARMENTS or not.

  Assistant Principal Snout knew that if he looked in Daisy's locker, and if there indeed was a furry creature inside, there was a definite possibility that it might not be wearing undergarments.

  But he also knew that if there was a furry creature in Daisy's locker, it was a clear violation of the NFA rule. And if Ulna Mandible found out that the NFA rule had been violated, she would shriek at him until his eardrums burst.

And the one thing Assistant Principal Snout feared *even more* than furry creatures without undergarments was THE SHRIEK OF ULNA MANDIBLE.

Not only that, but if Ulna Mandible learned that the NFA rule had been broken, she would probably sue the school for six million trillion dollars, and that would mean canceling the annual overnight campout and cutting back on field trips. Assistant Principal Snout loved the campout and field trips because on those days fewer germ-carrying students came to school.

So Assistant Principal Snout stepped forward, and with a hand covered by a blue latex glove opened Daisy's locker!

On the bottom of the locker was a ball of brown fur.

"What's that?" asked Assistant Principal Snout.

"An old sweater," said Wade.

Assistant Principal Snout quickly closed the locker. He was glad that Daisy wasn't breaking the NFA rule. He was also glad that there was no furry creature in her locker that might not be wearing an undergarment.

Assistant Principal Snout said to Barton Slugg, "I saw nothing in Daisy's locker that violated the NFA rule."

Then he walked away as quickly as he could.

After Assistant Principal Snout left, Barton Slugg turned to the Tardy Boys and Daisy and Al-Ian. "You didn't believe

I'd tell Assistant Principal Snout that there was a dog in your locker, but I did. Now either you invite me to your party *right now* or I'll get him to come back and open Daisy's locker again. Only next time, I'll poke that old dog and make him yelp. Then Assistant Principal Snout will know that it's not an old sweater."

Wade had to think fast. He didn't want Barton Slugg leaving trails of smelly slime through their party, but he also couldn't let Assistant Principal Snout find Wheezy in Daisy's locker. Suddenly he had an idea.

"Suppose we make a deal?" he asked.

Barton narrowed his eyes suspiciously. "What kind of deal?"

"This afternoon you're supposed to debate Leyton in Ms. Fitt's class," Wade said. "If my brother wins the debate, you promise to leave the dog alone. If you win the debate, we promise to invite you to *every* party for the rest of the year."

An evil smile appeared on Barton's face. Like the other kids at school, he knew that Leyton Tardy wasn't the brightest bulb in the candelabra. "It's a deal. The truth is, I don't care about your stupid dog. But I do want to be invited to every party. And I already know I'll win the debate this afternoon because I've been studying for days. I bet your brother hasn't spent a second preparing. He probably thinks the Constitution is some old warship and a colony is a place where ants live." Barton turned to Leyton. "When I see you at the debate this afternoon there's one thing you better be prepared for . . . losing."

SQUEEZING
WHEEZY

The bell rang and Barton headed for his next class, leaving a trail of slime behind him.

"We better get to class," said Wade.

"Wait," said Daisy. "In two periods someone has to take Wheezy outside again. But I can't because I'll be in the gym, setting up my model for the architectural competition."

"Then we'll do it," said Wade. He turned to Al-Ian. "Can you help us?"

"If I haven't been kidnapped by aliens," Al-Ian answered.

Wade and Leyton left their friends and went down the hall to their next class.

Two periods later they met in the same place.

"Wow, those two periods really went by fast," said Wade.

"They sure did," agreed Leyton. "It feels like we were just standing here a second ago."

The two brothers started to walk up the hall. When they turned the corner, their noses encountered the foul French cheese dog breath smell.

"It's gotten worse!" Leyton cried.

Kids were coming down the hall with their hands over their faces. Teachers held handkerchiefs over their noses while they sprayed air fresheners.

"Do we really have to go up there?" Leyton asked.

"Yes," said Wade.

Despite the odor, Leyton followed his brother up the hall. But he wasn't happy. Kids were streaming toward them like rats fleeing a stinking ship. Two girls were dragging Fibby Mandible while her eyes rolled around loosely in her head.

The Tardy Boys staggered forward. Suddenly they came across Al-Ian strolling along the hallway as if nothing was the matter. In addition to his black Velostat Thought-Screen Helmet and his Intergalactic Return Address Dog Tags, he was now wearing football shoulder pads covered with aluminum foil.

"Al-Ian, how can you just stroll along?"

Wade asked him. "Can't you smell the foul French cheese dog breath?"

Al-Ian pointed toward his nose. Stuffed into each nostril was a small wad of dark gray foam. "These are Alien Body Odor Protectors. When alien kidnappers come from faraway galaxies they don't always bathe regularly. It's well-known that after a trip of several million light-years some aliens get pretty ripe. Are you going to Daisy's locker to get Wheezy?"

"We're trying, but I don't know if I can make it," Leyton gasped.

"We must," Wade said. "For Daisy's sake."

Leyton coughed. "But the smell is too strong."

"We can do it!" Wade urged him. "Don't forget we are the Tardy Boys!"

"What's that got to do with this terrible stink?" asked Leyton.

"I don't know," answered Wade. "But it sounded good."

Leyton stopped. "Forget it! I'm tired of doing everything you tell me to do. I'm tired of being laughed at because my head isn't as thickly packed with brain cells as yours. If you're so smart, you should be able to come up with a better reason for me to let my nose face this kind of torture." He started back down the hall.

"Wait! Where are you going?" Wade cried. "We promised Daisy we would take care of Wheezy."

"You guys do it," Leyton said as he walked away. "I'll meet you outside as soon as I find some index cards."

Leyton turned the corner and disappeared. Suddenly the school's public address system crackled on: "*Attention, this is Assistant Principal Snout. A bad smell has* been detected in our school. Please do not be alarmed. While the smell may be awful, it is not harmful. I have asked our wonderful janitor, Olga Shotput, to look for the source of the smell. In the meantime, please continue to attend your regularly scheduled classes. If you feel that the smell is too strong, try not to breathe."

"If Olga starts looking in lockers, she'll find Wheezy," Al-Ian said.

"Then we must get to him first," insisted Wade.

Together they continued up the hall. The stink was so bad that the hallway was empty. They managed to get to Daisy's locker and open it. A thick haze of foul French cheese dog breath wafted out. The stench was so great it knocked Wade backward and sent him gagging and coughing.

"I can't do it!" Wade gasped. "The smell is too great!"

"Don't give up, Wade!" Al-Ian cried. "We must go through with it!"

Together they crawled back to the open locker.

"It's awful!" Wade groaned.

"I know!" gasped Al-Ian. "Even my Alien Body Odor Protectors are failing. This smell is worse than the body odor of the Putrid Aliens from the Planet Malodorous in the Skunk Galaxy!"

Wheezy lay curled in a ball in the bottom of the locker, surrounded by a blanket of loose dog hair.

"For a little dog, he sure does shed a lot," Al-Ian said.

Wade placed Wheezy in the cardboard box. Then he and Al-Ian ran to **THE** *not so* **SECRET DOOR TO THE OUTSIDE**. They burst through it and fell to the ground, gasping for fresh air.

By the time Al-Ian and Wade recovered from the horrible odor, Leyton had found index cards and returned. He stepped through **THE** *not so* **SECRET DOOR TO THE OUTSIDE** and looked into the cardboard box where Wheezy was rolled into a ball, sleeping. The bottom of the box was covered with fur.

"I've never seen a dog shed so much," he said. "Do you think there's something wrong with him?"

Wade and Al-Ian looked into the box. The fur on Wheezy's body was starting to look thin. In a few spots wrinkled pink old pug dog skin was beginning to show through.

"Maybe he's shedding because it's too warm in Daisy's locker," Wade guessed.

"Or maybe he's shedding because his body has been invaded by Flea Aliens from the Planet Itch in the Scratchy Galaxy," suggested Al-Ian.

Wade and Leyton stared at their friend as if his brain had been taken over by the Airhead Aliens from the Planet Ignoramous in the Dumb Galaxy.

"Let's get Wheezy to do his business," Wade said and lifted the sleeping dog out of the box. Leyton straightened the old dog's legs, and Wade set him down on the grass. Wheezy stood on his stiff little legs, eyes closed, fast asleep.

Wade kneeled next to him on the grass and whispered, "Wheezy, go."

Wheezy didn't move.

"Wheezy, go!" Wade whispered again.

Wheezy didn't budge.

Wade looked up at Leyton and Al-Ian. "What should I do?"

The other boys shrugged. Wade tried whispering in Wheezy's ear again, but the little old pug dog didn't respond.

Wade shook his head. "I can't get him to go and we can't stay out here forever. We have to get to our next class."

"Then there's only one thing we can do," said Leyton. "If Wheezy won't go by himself, we'll have to squeeze it out of him." He reached down with both hands to grab the old pug dog around the tummy and squeeze!

QUEASY WHEEZY

Wade had a feeling Wheezy was not going to enjoy being squeezed.

"Wait!" he said. "Before you try to squeeze it out of him, let me see if I can find Daisy. Maybe she can tell us why we're having so much trouble getting Wheezy to go."

Wade dashed back inside and headed

down the hall to the gym where long rows of tables had been set up. On the tables were the models of famous buildings that students had entered for the architectural competition. Towering over all the other models was Fibby Mandible's White House.

A few rows behind Fibby's model, Wade found Daisy setting up her model of the state capitol.

"Wade, what are you doing here?" she asked.

"We're having a problem with Wheezy," Wade whispered. "We can't get him to do his business."

"Did you whisper in his ear?" asked Daisy.

"Yes," said Wade.

"Then I can't imagine why he won't go," Daisy said.

"Neither can I, but if we can't get Wheezy to go, Leyton says he'll have to squeeze it out of him," said Wade.

Daisy's eyes widened with alarm. "Oh, no! You mustn't squeeze Wheezy! Squeezing Wheezy makes him queasy!"

Wade and Daisy rushed out of the gym and down the hall. Daisy's bare feet slapped against the tile floor and her baggy yellow tie-dyed sundress billowed. As they ran, Wade thought he saw something strange out of the corner of his eye. It looked like someone wearing a big white spacesuit with a round glass helmet on top. Wade would have stopped to take a closer look, but Daisy was running as fast as she could and he wanted to keep up.

They went through **THE** *not so* **SECRET DOOR TO THE OUTSIDE**. Leyton was holding Wheezy as if he was about to squeeze!

"Oh, please, please, don't squeeze Wheezy, you'll make him queasy!" Daisy pleaded.

"And queasy Wheezy will make Fibby sneezy!" Al-Ian exclaimed.

"The idea made *me* feel queasy, too," Leyton admitted as he put Wheezy back down on his stiff little legs on the grass. The old pug dog's eyes were still closed. "But I didn't know what else to do."

Daisy kneeled next to Wheezy and whispered "Go, Wheezy, go." At the same time, she tickled the old pug dog's throat. With his eyes still closed, Wheezy lifted his back leg and went.

"See?" Daisy said, standing up. "That wasn't so hard."

"But you tickled his throat," Wade said.

Daisy brought her hand to her mouth in surprise. "You're right! I'm so sorry! I forgot to tell you about that!"

"It's okay," said Wade. "The good news is that Wheezy did his business. Let's put him back in the box and go."

Al-Ian was standing closest to the door. He reached for the handle and pulled, but the door stayed shut. "It won't open."

"Let me see," said Wade. The door had shut completely. That meant someone had removed the piece of paper he'd jammed in the doorway to keep it open. Wade wondered who would do such a terrible thing. Then he looked through the window and saw buckteeth.

THE RETURN OF ULNA MANDIBLE

On the other side of the window Barton Slugg held up the wad of paper. He had a mean smile on his lips.

"Why is he smiling like that?" asked Al-Ian.

"He knows he's got us between a rock and a hard place," answered Wade.

Leyton looked around. "I don't see a rock OR a hard place."

"It's just a saying," Wade said and signaled for Barton to open the door.

Barton opened it a little. "Having fun with your smelly old dog?" he asked, then turned to Leyton. "Ready to lose the debate this afternoon and invite me to every party for the rest of the year?"

"He hasn't lost the debate yet," said Wade. "So why don't you let us in before we're late for our next class?"

Barton stepped back from the doorway. Daisy went in first. Then came Leyton, carrying Wheezy in the box, and then Wade. Al-Ian, with his black Velostat Thought-Screen Helmet, Intergalactic Return Address Dog Tags, Alien Body Odor Protectors, and shoulder pads covered with aluminum foil followed last.

Barton blocked Al-Ian's path. "What's your problem?"

"I don't have a problem," answered Al-Ian while Daisy and the Tardy Boys hurried ahead.

"Why are you wearing all that junk and those shoulder pads covered with aluminum foil?" asked Barton.

"Because alien kidnappers trace their victims with body heat sensors," Al-Ian explained. "The aluminum foil on these shoulder pads deflects alien body heat sensor rays."

"You are one sick puppy," said Barton Slugg.

Meanwhile, the Tardy Boys and Daisy turned the corner and found Ulna Mandible coming toward them wearing a large white spacesuit with a glass helmet. In her gloved hands was a small, black plastic gadget with red and green lights on it.

As soon as the Tardy Boys and Daisy got near Ulna, the lights on the gadget began to flash brightly. From inside the glass helmet, Ulna shouted, "*Stop!*"

The Tardy Boys and Daisy stopped. "Why are you wearing that spacesuit?" asked Wade.

"*It is not a spacesuit!*" Ulna Mandible yelled. "*It is an Anti-Allergen Outfit. It will prevent any animal fur, milk, nuts, chocolate, vegetables, berries, dust, pollen, smoke, math, or gym germs from getting on my clothes. That way I will be sure not to bring home anything that might cause my daughter Fibula to have an allergic reaction.*"

The lights on the gadget in Ulna Mandible's hands kept flashing.

"What's that thing?" asked Wade.

"*It is an Animal Fur Detector!*" screamed

Ulna. "*And right now it's detecting animal fur very near by.*"

The closer Ulna came, the more brightly the lights on the Animal Fur Detector flashed. Fibby's mother focused on the cardboard box in Leyton's arms.

"*What's in that box?*" she screeched.

Leyton stepped back fearfully.

Ulna stepped forward. The Animal Fur Detector kept flashing. "*I said, what's in that box!?*"

"Nothing!" Leyton stammered. "It's just an empty box. A lonely, empty box that looked like it needed a friend. And I am a boy who makes friends with boxes. In fact, some of my best friends are boxes. Big boxes, little boxes, square boxes, and round boxes."

"*Are you insane?*" Ulna Mandible shrieked.

THE SHRIEK OF ULNA MANDIBLE woke Wheezy. Inside the box in Leyton's arms, the old pug dog yawned and stretched his stiff little legs. When Wheezy's legs touched the cardboard, they made a scratching sound.

"*What made that sound?!*" Ulna screamed.

"Nothing!" Leyton yelped.

"*You're lying!*" Ulna shouted. "*Something moved inside that box!*"

Ulna dropped the Animal Fur Detector and tried to grab the box from Leyton. Just then, someone cried excitedly, "You're here! I'm so glad you've finally come!"

KIDNAPPED
AT LAST!

Everyone spun around. Al-Ian was running toward them with his arms spread wide. His black Velostat Thought-Screen Helmet had blown back from his head. His aluminum-foil covered shoulder pads were flapping and one of the Alien Body Odor Protectors was falling out of his nose.

"I'm so happy to see you!" He threw his

arms around Ulna Mandible and gave her a big hug.

"*Why are you happy to see me?*" Ulna Mandible screamed.

"Because you're an alien!" said Al-Ian.

"*No I'm not!*" Ulna Mandible screeched.

"Oh, yes, you are!" cried Al-Ian. "I was so worried you'd never come!"

While Ulna Mandible was being distracted, Wade motioned to Leyton to open the box. He took out Wheezy, hurried to Daisy's locker, and quietly placed the dog inside.

Meanwhile Ulna pulled off the glass helmet and screeched, "*I'm not an alien! I'm Ulna Mandible!*"

Al-Ian stepped back, stunned. "Can't you *please* be an alien?" His eyes began to fill with tears.

"No!" Ulna Mandible ripped the box out

of Leyton's hands. She tore it open. Pieces of cardboard flew everywhere, but the box was empty.

"*Where is it?!*" she shrieked.

"Where is what?" asked Leyton.

"*The furry animal,*" screeched Ulna.

"We told you the box was empty," said Wade.

"Are you *sure* you're not an alien?" Al-Ian asked, wiping the tears from his reddened eyes.

"*Yes!*" Ulna Mandible grabbed the Animal Fur Detector and stormed away.

The Tardy Boys, Daisy, and Al-Ian stayed behind to pick up the torn pieces of cardboard. Al-Ian sniffed sadly.

"There's one thing I don't understand," Wade said to him. "If you thought Ulna Mandible was an alien, why were you so happy to see her?"

"Because if she was an alien it would mean that I'm not a total nut job," Al-Ian explained.

"We don't think you're a total nut job," said Daisy.

"Really?" Al-Ian asked.

"No," said Wade.

"Not even a semi-nut job?" asked Al-Ian.

"Well, maybe," admitted Daisy. "But at least you're a nice semi-nut job. We like nice semi-nut jobs a lot more than mean normal people."

Al-Ian breathed a sigh of relief. "Thank you. I feel much better now. You guys are the best friends a semi-nut job ever had."

FRENCH CHEESE OR TOE CHEESE?

It was time for the double-period debate. The Tardy Boys, Al-Ian, and Daisy went into Ms. Fitt's social studies class. The room seemed unusually quiet and Wade quickly saw why: Sitting in the back of the classroom was Principal Stratemeyer and two other important-looking people. Everyone waited silently for Ms. Fitt to arrive. Finally the door swung open and she stepped into the room wearing her bright yellow sweater, orange felt skirt, and green-and-white cowboy boots. When Ms. Fitt walked, her curly red hair bounced on her shoulders. She stopped in front of the classroom.

"Hello, class," she said in a cheerful voice. "As you've probably noticed, we have some very special visitors today. In addition to Principal Stratemeyer, we have two members of the school board. They are here to observe the wonderful work we are doing and I know that you will all be on your best behavior."

Ms. Fitt pointed at the debate jar filled with index cards on her desk. "Today is Leyton's and Barton's turn to debate. As you know, each can pick a partner to team with. Leyton will choose first."

"I want Al-Ian," said Leyton.

Ms. Fitt turned to Barton. "And who would you like?"

"Fibby," said Barton.

Fibby Mandible glowed with pride. Everyone knew that Barton had chosen her because she always got the best grades in the class. This, of course, was because her mother, Ulna, did most of her homework, and hired tutors to help her prepare for every test.

"Very good," said Ms. Fitt. "Barton will pick a card from the debate jar. You will be required to debate whatever topic is stated on the card."

Barton went to the front of the classroom leaving a trail of slime that smelled like unwashed feet. Kids pinched their noses. Even Ms. Fitt fanned her face while Barton reached into the debate jar and pulled out an index card.

Barton began to read: "The topic of my debate against Leyton will be . . ." he stopped reading and frowned. His eyes darted nervously toward Ms. Fitt and then toward the back of the room where Principal Stratemeyer and the members of the school board were sitting.

"What does it say, Barton?" Ms. Fitt said.

"Ahem." Barton cleared his throat and said, "I think there's been a mistake."

Now it was Ms. Fitt's turn to glance nervously at Principal Stratemeyer. She did not want any mistakes on the day of her annual review. "Barton," she said, "I hand picked these topics very carefully. You may not like the topic you've chosen, but it's definitely not a mistake."

Barton looked down at the card again and then back at Ms. Fitt. "But I really think it is," he whispered.

"No, Barton, there can't be a mistake," said Ms. Fitt. "Please let me see the card."

Barton handed her the debate card. Suddenly it was her turn to frown. "It's not possible," she muttered to herself. "It's just not possible."

Ms. Fitt stared at the card, then reached into the jar and took out some other cards. Her mouth fell open as she read them. Meanwhile the class began to fidget and whisper.

"Is there a problem, Ms. Fitt?" Principal Stratemeyer asked.

The teacher stiffened. "Oh, no, sir. There's no problem. None whatsoever." She handed the card back to Barton. "Go ahead."

Barton scowled. "But —"

"You heard me," Ms. Fitt said firmly. "Go ahead!"

Barton faced the class again. "The topic of my debate against Leyton will be —" He looked down at the card, then back at the class. "Which smells and tastes worse? French cheese or toe cheese?"

AN
EXPERT
WITNESS

Suddenly Wade realized that Leyton had snuck into Ms. Fitt's classroom and changed the cards in the debate jar to topics he knew something about. Wade smiled proudly. Maybe there was more than butterflies in his brother's head after all!

To perform the debate, Leyton, Al-Ian, Barton, and Fibby sat facing one another at a table in the front of the classroom. Ms. Fitt spoke to the debate teams: "Barton, which side of the debate do you wish to take?"

Barton and Fibby whispered to each other. Meanwhile Daisy passed a note to Wade which said:

> It's been an hour and a half since we last walked Wheezy!

Wade knew it was time to walk Wheezy again, but he had no idea how to get out of class. By now, Barton and Fibby had come to an agreement.

"We wish to argue that French cheese smells and tastes worse than toe cheese," said Barton.

"Very well," said Ms. Fitt. "Both teams

will now prepare their opening arguments."

While Leyton whispered with Al-Ian and Barton whispered with Fibby, Ms. Fitt smiled weakly at Principal Stratemeyer and the school board members in the back of the room.

"Leyton," the teacher finally said, "please give your opening argument."

Leyton rose to his feet. His hands were trembling. "Okay, I have to admit that French cheese tastes and smells pretty darn bad."

A surprised gasp rippled through the class.

"Leyton," Ms. Fitt said, "are you sure you want to start that way? It sounds like you are agreeing with Barton that French cheese tastes and smells worse than toe cheese."

"What I meant to say," said Leyton, "is that French cheese may taste and smell pretty darn bad *to us,* but *we're not French.* The thing is, the French *love* smelly cheese. They've invented more than two hundred different kinds of foul-smelling cheese. Therefore, while we may think French cheese is awful, the French think it tastes and smells great."

The class nodded its approval, but in the back Principal Stratemeyer sat with his arms crossed and a frown on his face. Ms. Fitt turned to Barton. "You may now present your opening argument."

Barton stood up. "I'd like to remind everyone that Leyton began by admitting that French cheese tastes and smells pretty bad, okay? So maybe the French don't think that their cheese stinks, but are there any French people around here?

No. They're all down in South America, or wherever they come from. We're not arguing about what the French think tastes and smells bad. We're arguing about what we Americans think tastes and smells bad. And I believe that most true Americans think French cheese tastes and smells worse than toe cheese."

Barton sat down and Leyton stood up. "I disagree. I'm an American and here in America we have something called the Constitution. And the First Amendment of the Constitution guarantees freedom of speech. And I figure if it can guarantee what you say, it can guarantee what you smell and taste. And I put forth that French cheese *tastes and smells* better than toe cheese."

Ms. Fitt clapped happily, mostly because Leyton had mentioned the United States

Constitution and the First Amendment, which is the kind of stuff teachers liked to hear. Leyton sat down, but Barton did not stand up. Instead, he and Fibby began a whispered debate of their own.

Daisy passed another note to Wade:

> If we don't walk Wheezy right away there's going to be a mess in the bottom of my locker!

Wade nodded back at Daisy, but he still couldn't figure out how to get out of the class. Meanwhile, Barton stood up. "Ms. Fitt. I believe I can offer conclusive testimony that French cheese smells and tastes worse than toe cheese."

"Do you understand that in order to introduce testimony you must have an expert witness?" Ms. Fitt asked.

"I do," said Barton.

"And that in order for an expert witness to do this, he or she must swear under oath that he or she has actually tasted both French cheese and toe cheese?"

"I do," said Barton.

Surprised murmurs ran through the class. In the back, the members of the review committee leaned forward in their chairs. Leyton was sweating bullets. No one had expected Barton to produce an expert witness!

Barton said, "My witness is . . . Fibby Mandible."

Leyton jumped to his feet. "I object! How can Fibby be an expert witness when she's also Barton's debating partner?"

"It doesn't matter," Barton argued. "As an expert witness she'll have to testify under oath."

Leyton quickly turned to Ms. Fitt. "You can't allow it!"

The teacher rubbed her chin thoughtfully. "We'll take a five-minute recess while I decide what to do. Those of you who need to get a drink of water or use the bathroom may do so now."

A moment later, Leyton, Wade, Al-Ian and Daisy were racing down the hall toward Daisy's locker.

"How am I going to win my debate against Barton?" asked Leyton.

"We'll worry about that after we take care of Wheezy," said Wade.

They entered the hallway where Daisy's locker was. Something was different. "It doesn't smell like foul French cheese dog breath anymore," said Al-Ian.

Daisy got to her locker and opened it. "Oh, no!" she cried. "Wheezy's gone!"

WHEEZY, DOG MAGICIAN

"Look!" Wade pointed into Daisy's locker. "There's a note!"

Lying at the bottom of the locker was a small piece of paper. Daisy picked it up. "Oh, no!"

"What does it say?" asked Leyton.

"'If you ever want to see your dog again, you better invite Barton Slugg to your parties whether or not he wins the debate,'" Daisy read.

"I wonder who wrote it?" said Leyton.

"Barton wrote it, you idiot," said Wade.

"Wouldn't he have written, 'If you ever want to see your dog again, you better invite *me* to your parties'?" Leyton asked.

"No, because then we wouldn't know who 'me' is," said Wade.

"I know who you are," said Leyton. "You're my brother."

Wade groaned. Leyton may have had the brains to plant that index card in the debate jar, but he was still as dumb as a speed bump.

"I can't believe Barton did this," Al-Ian said. "He said he'd leave Wheezy out of it."

"Evil slimeballs don't keep their word," said Wade. "That's why they're evil slimeballs."

"Boys," Daisy interrupted, "we have to go look for Wheezy right now."

"That way." Wade pointed down the hall.

"Why that way?" asked Leyton.

"Because that's the direction with the most kids holding their noses and looking like they want to barf," said Wade.

He was right. Pale-looking kids staggered down the hall with their fingers pinching their noses. As the Tardy Boys, Al-Ian, and Daisy started up the hall the terrible odor grew worse.

Soon the Tardy Boys and their friends were also stumbling and feeling faint. Outside the gym doors the odor was so strong that Leyton moaned, "I don't think I can continue!"

"But we must!" cried Daisy and pushed through the doors. Inside, the gym was empty except for the rows of tables

123

covered by models of famous buildings. The rich, pungent odor was as thick as fog.

"It's the mother of all odors!" Al-Ian groaned.

"Wheezy must be here somewhere," gasped Wade.

"But the gym's so big," said Daisy. "And he could be anywhere."

"No, wait!" Leyton said excitedly. "I know *exactly* where he is!"

THE YELLOW HOUSE

"How do you know?" asked Daisy.

"I just do," said Leyton.

"Do you see him?" asked Wade.

"No," said Leyton.

"Did you hear him?" asked Al-Ian.

"No," said Leyton.

"Well, we know you can smell him, but that can't help," said Wade. "Because the smell is everywhere."

"No, it's not that, either," said Leyton.

"Then how do you know where Wheezy is?" asked Daisy.

"Look at Fibby Mandible's model," Leyton said.

They all looked at Fibby's White House.

Only it was no longer white.

It was now yellow.

"We're too late," Wade said sadly.

"But at least we found him!" Daisy cried happily and ran toward the White House that was now yellow.

"*Attention staff and students!*" Suddenly Assistant Principal Snout's voice boomed over the public address system. "*The source of the terrible smell has been traced to the gym. Everyone in the gym must evacuate immediately! You must leave the gym now!*"

Before Daisy could reach Wheezy, silver

medalist janitor Olga Shotput rushed into the gym carrying a broom and wearing a gas mask.

"Out! Out! You must get out!" With her broom Olga began to shoo the Tardy Boys and their friends out of the gym.

"But I have to get something," Daisy protested.

"Not now!" Olga insisted. "Assistant Principal Snout says you must leave! You must do what Assistant Principal Snout says. That is an order!"

"But —" Daisy tried to argue.

"No buts allowed! This area is officially off limits to buts!" Olga waved Daisy and the others toward the gym doors. "Go! Take your buts somewhere else!"

"But what about Wheezy?" Daisy whimpered in a soft voice Olga couldn't hear.

Wade took Daisy's hand and led her out of the gym. "We have to go back to the debate anyway. Don't worry. We'll get Wheezy back somehow."

A DEAD CRITTER

When the Tardy Boys, Daisy, and Al-Ian got back to the classroom, Ms. Fitt was asking Fibby: "Even though you are Barton's debate partner, do you promise to tell the truth as an expert witness on the subject of toe and French cheeses?"

"I do," replied Fibby.

Ms. Fitt turned to Leyton. "I have decided to overrule your objection,

Leyton. Barton may question his expert witness."

Barton clasped his hands behind his back and faced Fibby. "Ms. Mandible," he said. "Have you ever eaten potato chips with your toes?"

The class went silent. Expert Witness Fibula Mandible sat up straight in her chair.

"Yes," she answered.

A collective gasp fluttered through the classroom.

"One day I was sitting on the floor watching TV and eating a bowl of potato chips," Fibby testified. "I was really bored so I decided to see if I could pick one up with my toes and eat it."

"And could you?" asked Barton.

"The first few potato chips broke," said Fibby. "But after a while I was able to do it."

"And did this lead to your actually eating toe cheese?" Barton asked.

"Yes," Fibby said. "Potato chips are greasy and after you've eaten a few with your toes, they start to get greasy, too. You know how people lick potato chip grease off their fingers? It's the same with your toes. And when you lick potato chip grease off your toes, you can't help but lick off some toe cheese as well."

"Gross!" someone groaned.

"I'm gonna barf!" someone else moaned.

More groans and moans rippled through the classroom. *Bang!* Ms. Fitt took off her green-and-white cowboy boot and banged it against the desktop. "Order!"

"Now, Ms. Mandible," Barton said. "You have testified that you have tasted toe cheese. Have you also tasted French cheese?"

"Yes, I have," answered Fibby.

"And in your expert opinion, which smells and tastes worse?" asked Barton.

"In my opinion, French cheese both smells and tastes worse than toe cheese."

Barton nodded gravely. "Thank you for your testimony, Ms. Mandible." He sat down and crossed his arms, smiling smugly at Leyton.

"I must say that while I am totally grossed out, that was indeed convincing testimony," Ms. Fitt said. "Leyton, you may cross examine the witness."

"*Attention staff and students!*" Assistant Principal Snout's voice suddenly boomed over the public address system. "*The source of the terrible smell has been discovered and will be removed from school. The gym has been reopened. Please return to your normal schedule.*"

Daisy let out a loud gasp. Meanwhile, Leyton gave Wade a pleading look as if begging for help with the debate.

Wade had an idea and raised his hand. "Ms. Fitt? On TV whenever one side brings in a surprise witness, the judge usually gives the other side time to prepare a rebuttal. I think it's only fair that my brother have a few minutes in private to prepare."

Ms. Fitt turned to Barton. "I think Wade's suggestion is a fair one. We'll take another short recess."

Barton shrugged confidently. He was certain that there was no way Leyton could win the debate now that Fibby had given her expert testimony. "Fine with me."

Wade stood up. "We'll be right back."

Once again, the Tardy Boys and their friends dashed out of class and into the hall.

"Why are we running?" asked Leyton. "I thought we were going to prepare for my rebuttal."

"After we find Wheezy!" Wade said.

"They're taking him away!" Daisy cried.

"But where?" asked Al-Ian.

"Olga will know," Wade said. "She's the one who must've found him."

The Tardy Boys and their friends hurried to the janitor's closet. A sticky note on the door read:

I have gone to the woods behind the school to bury the dead and very smelly critter.

"Dead?!" Daisy cried.

"Or just asleep," said Al-Ian.

"Either way, we've got to stop her!" Daisy started to run down the hall.

While she and Leyton went ahead, Wade whispered something in Al-Ian's ear. Al-Ian went in another direction and Wade ran to catch up to Leyton and Daisy. They went through **THE** *not so* **SECRET DOOR TO THE OUTSIDE**, then crossed the football field and ran behind the bleachers to the woods. As they reached the trees they heard the scrape of a shovel digging into the ground.

"There!" Wade pointed to a small clearing where Olga was digging a hole. On the ground near her was a trumpet case.

"Stop!" Daisy cried and ran toward her.

Olga looked up. "Why should I stop? Who sent you? What are your orders?"

"Uh, we have been ordered by our science teacher, Mr. Beeker, to find out what the source of the terrible odor was," Wade said.

Olga pointed at the trumpet case. "A dead critter."

Daisy reached down to open the case.

"Don't touch it!" Olga yelled.

Daisy straightened up. "Why not?"

"You must have a principal's permission," said the janitor.

Daisy stared longingly at the trumpet case. "But how do you know it . . . I mean, the critter . . . is really dead?" she asked.

"Nothing that smells that bad could possibly be alive," said Olga.

"But you don't know for sure," Daisy said.

"Don't know WHAT for sure?" someone screamed.

Olga and Daisy spun around. Wade quickly grabbed Leyton and whispered in his ear. Coming toward them through the woods was Assistant Principal Snout and Ulna Mandible! Assistant Principal Snout was wearing a white breathing mask, blue latex gloves, and yellow foam earplugs. Ulna Mandible was wearing her glass helmet and Anti-Allergen Outfit.

"*We heard that the source of the terrible smell was a dead critter!*" Ulna Mandible screeched. "*What I want to know is, was it a FURRY dead critter?*"

"Does she have permission to look?" Olga asked Assistant Principal Snout.

"Yes," said Assistant Principal Snout.

Olga pointed at the trumpet case. "See for yourself."

Ulna Mandible stepped toward the case. Wade knew what would happen if Ulna looked inside. There was only one thing he could do.

WE WILL SURELY MISS HIM

With his foot Wade slid the trumpet case into the hole Olga had just dug!

Thump! The trumpet case fell to the bottom of the hole.

"*What are you doing?!*" Daisy and Ulna Mandible both screamed.

"We are burying this poor, sad, smelly critter," Wade said with a sniff and

dumped a shovelful of dirt on the
case.

"But I *need to see if it was a furry dead
critter!*" screamed Ulna Mandible.

Wade dumped another shovelful of dirt
on the case. "Sorry. You know what they
say: It is disrespectful to disturb the dead."
Wade lowered his head. "Let us all observe
a moment of silence for the poor dead smelly
critter. Then I will recite a memorial poem."

Everyone hung their heads for a
moment of silence. Then Wade recited:

> *Here lies a dead critter*
> *I wish I knew him better*
> *It's true he smelled pretty bad*
> *That he's dead makes some people glad*
> *But I will surely miss him*
> *Although I'd never kiss him.*

Wade handed the shovel to Olga, who dumped more dirt into the hole. Tears rolled down Daisy's cheeks. Wade put his arm around her shoulder. Soon Olga had filled the hole with dirt. Somewhere under the dirt was the trumpet case.

Daisy began to sob and shake.

"*Why are you blubbering over a smelly dead critter?*" Ulna Mandible screeched.

"Because . . ." Daisy sniffed. "Smelly or not, it was a critter and somebody probably loved it. Even smelly critters have mothers, you know."

"Yes," Wade agreed solemnly. "And that concludes our ceremony. It is now time for all of us to return to school and allow this poor smelly critter to rest in peace."

"*But what if it was a furry critter?*" Ulna Mandible yelled. "*What if it is breaking the NFA rule?*"

"I'm afraid that is no longer possible," said Assistant Principal Snout. "The NFA rule states that no furry animals are allowed *on* school property. It doesn't matter whether the smelly dead critter in the trumpet case was furry or not because he is no longer *on* school property. He is now *in* school property."

"Bravo!" Wade clapped. Daisy did not clap because she was heartbroken. Assistant Principal Snout checked his watch and gave Wade and Daisy a stern look. "Late for class as usual. Go to your next period, now!"

"But —" Daisy began to protest.

"No buts allowed!" yelled Olga.

Wade kept his arm around Daisy's shoulders as they walked away from the little grave.

"Don't worry," he whispered. "Wheezy's okay."

Daisy's eyes widened and her jaw fell. "How? And what happened to Leyton?"

"He took Wheezy out of the trumpet case when the others turned to look at Assistant Principal Snout and Ulna Mandible," Wade said. "Right now Wheezy is probably sound asleep in your locker."

"Oh, Wade!" Daisy hugged him. "Thank you! And I want to hug Leyton, too. Where is he?"

At that moment, Leyton was sitting at the debate table in Ms. Fitt's class looking miserable. Principal Stratemeyer and the other members of the review committee were tapping their feet and drumming their fingers impatiently, and Ms. Fitt looked very unhappy. Only Barton Slugg and Fibby Mandible looked happy.

"If you don't start your cross examination

of the witness right now, I will have to disqualify you," Ms. Fitt told Leyton.

Wade and Daisy entered the room and went to their desks. Leyton gave his brother a dismal glance. He had no idea how to do a cross examination. It looked like Barton was going to win the debate and be invited to their parties forever.

LEYTON HAS AN IDEA!

Suddenly, the door burst open and Al-Ian raced in with a bag of potato chips he'd gotten from the lunchroom. He quickly sat down next to Leyton and whispered in his ear. Leyton jumped to his feet.

"Ms. Fitt," he said. "While we do not wish to cast doubt on the honesty of the expert witness, we do wish to make sure her testimony is accurate. Therefore, we would like her to demonstrate that what she says is true."

"That sounds fair," said Ms. Fitt.

Leyton held the bag of potato chips toward Fibby. "Fibby Mandible, you have testified under oath that you can eat potato chips with your toes. I would ask you to show us this is true."

Fibby sighed loudly and rolled her eyes. She opened the bag of potato chips and placed them on the debate table. Then she slid her chair back and took off her shoe and sock. The class craned their necks forward to watch. Even the members of the review committee seemed more interested.

Fibby swung her leg up and bent

her knee so that her foot was flat on the tabletop. She moved her foot toward the potato chips. Then she bent her toes and tried to pick one up. *Crack!* The potato chip broke. The class gasped.

Fibby pursed her lips with determination and tried again. This time she managed to get her toes to close over a chip without breaking it. The class held its breath as Fibby grasped her ankle with her hands and slowly drew her foot toward her face with her toes still clutching the potato chip.

Leyton's heart was beating hard. His breathing became short, and little dots of perspiration began to bead up on his forehead. If Fibby managed to get that potato chip into her mouth, then Barton would win the debate!

Fibby pulled her foot nearer and nearer to her face. The potato chip came closer and closer to her mouth. Fibby parted her lips and . . .

The potato chip fell to the floor!

The class groaned. Leyton felt a wave of relief. Ms. Fitt gave Fibby a stern look.

"I can do it!" Fibby insisted. "It's just hard in front of so many people. I need one more chance."

Leyton rose to his feet. "I wish to lodge a formal protest. Fibby testified that she could eat potato chips with her toes and that was how she knew what toe cheese tasted like. She has now failed twice. How many more times are we supposed to let her try? How long are we supposed to sit here and wait?"

Barton jumped to his feet. "I insist that she have one more try."

"We will give Fibby one more chance," Ms. Fitt decided.

Fibby's foot hovered over the potato chips. Once again she managed to pick one up with her toes. Once again she slowly pulled her foot toward her mouth. Once again she parted her lips and brought her toes closer.

Closer . . .

Closer!

Fibby opened her mouth wide. The potato chip and all five toes disappeared inside!

The class moaned with grossed-out amazement as Fibby not only ate the potato chip but sucked on her toes as well!

"There!" Barton Slugg cried. "That's absolute proof that Fibby can eat potato chips with her toes! Therefore she is qualified to be an expert witness on which smells and tastes worse, French cheese or toe cheese!"

"I'm sorry, Leyton," Ms. Fitt said. "But it appears that you have lost the debate. The good news is that you debated well and were prepared for your subject so you will pass the class."

Leyton glanced sadly at his brother and Daisy. Yes, it was good news that he would not face the AWFUL FATE OF FLUNKDOM. But the bad news was that they would now have to invite Barton to every party they threw. Unless . . .

Leyton tried to think harder than he'd ever thought before. So hard that the butterflies in his head whirled around as if they were in a blender.

But a blender doesn't blend butterflies. It blends food. And food either tastes good or bad. Suddenly, Leyton had an idea!

THE END
(MAY BE COMING SOON)

"Wait!" Leyton jumped to his feet. His knees were shaking and his heart was pounding. He had one chance. And it was a slim one. "All Fibby did was prove that she could eat potato chips with her toes. She did not actually *prove* that French cheese tastes and smells worse than toe cheese. I have seen many television commercials. In the real world these things are decided in *blind* taste tests where the person is not allowed to see what they're eating, but is only allowed to smell and taste it."

Barton jumped up. "I object!" he shouted. "This is not the real world. It is school!"

"I agree with Leyton," said Ms. Fitt, "but in order to perform such a test, you would have to get some toe cheese."

Leyton looked around the room at his classmates. "I believe that there is an ample supply of toe cheese on hand. Or, I guess I should say, on foot."

"You would also need actual French cheese," said Ms. Fitt.

Leyton nodded at Daisy, who opened her backpack and took out the plastic container of Camembert.

"Ms. Fitt," said Leyton. "I have actual, real French cheese."

"All right," said Ms. Fitt. "And whose toe cheese would you like to compare it to?"

Leyton glanced around the room. His eyes stopped on the one person who was guaranteed to have the creamiest, mushiest, smelliest toe cheese of all: Barton Slugg!

Fibby was blindfolded. On the table before her were two potato chips. On one was a piece of Camembert cheese. On the other was Barton Slugg's toe cheese.

With the blindfold covering her eyes, Fibby bent down and sniffed one chip, then the other. Back and forth went her nose from one chip to the next.

The class held its breath.

Fibby's nose kept going back and forth.

Principal Stratemeyer and the other members of the review committee held their breath.

Fibby's nose stopped over the potato chip upon which was spread the creamy stinky cheese from Barton Slugg's toes. Fibby took a deep whiff. Her nose wrinkled and her lips bent into a frown. She reached down . . . *and picked up the other chip!*

"You see!" Leyton cried. "That proves conclusively that French cheese smells and tastes better than toe cheese!"

Wade jumped in the air and pumped his fist! This meant they would not have to invite Barton Slugg to any of their parties.

"You idiot!" Barton screamed at Fibby.

"I couldn't help it!" Fibby cried, pulling off the blindfold. "The French cheese smelled bad, but your toe cheese smelled worse!"

"That concludes the debate," Ms. Fitt announced. "I declare Leyton Tardy the winner."

The class cheered. In the back of the classroom the review committee led by Principal Stratemeyer stood up. Ms. Fitt bit her lip nervously.

"Ms. Fitt," Principal Stratemeyer said, "that was one of the most —"

Brrriiinnnnggg! The bell rang. Kids began to stream out of the class. Leyton started to leave, but Wade grabbed him. "Wait," Wade whispered. "I want to hear what Principal Stratemeyer says."

The class hurried out. Ms. Fitt stayed behind, rubbing her hands and looking worried.

Principal Stratemeyer began again, "As I was saying, Ms. Fitt, that was one of the most . . . *impressive* demonstrations of student debate, logic, and reasoning I have ever seen. Congratulations! You have passed your annual review!"

Ms. Fitt clutched her heart with relief.

"Way to go, Ms. Fitt!" Wade cheered.

By now most of the class had left the room.

"Where's Daisy?" Al-Ian asked.

Leyton looked around. "She was here a second ago."

"I know where she must have gone!" Wade rushed out of the room.

(STILL NOT QUITE) THE END

They ran through the halls toward Daisy's locker. Once again, the rich, pungent odor of foul French cheese dog breath hung in the air. They found Daisy kneeling on the floor before her open locker. A pale, skinny, nearly hairless creature lay cradled in her arms. Except for little bits of fur left on his head and tail, Wheezy was all wrinkled bare skin.

"Is he okay?" Leyton asked, pinching his nose to keep it from jumping off his face and running away.

Daisy nodded.

"What happened to his fur?" asked Al-Ian, as he readjusted his Alien Body Odor Protectors.

"We don't know," said Wade. "It's been falling out all day."

Daisy hugged the little sleeping dog. "I don't care about his fur. I'm just happy he's okay. Wheezy's a nice old dog and he never hurt anyone."

Suddenly they heard the sound of footsteps. Coming down the hall toward them were:

1) Assistant Principal Snout, who hated everything that might carry germs, including students and little old pug dogs.

2) Ulna Mandible, who hated everything that might make her daughter have an allergic reaction, including little old pug dogs.

3) Barton Slugg, who hated everything that made him unpopular, including little old pug dogs.

4) Fibby Mandible, who just plain hated everything (including little old pug dogs).

"Oh, no!" cried Leyton. "This time we're really, totally, completely, and utterly busted for good!"

Daisy quickly put Wheezy back into her locker and shut it. But it was too late.

"We can smell what's in your locker, young lady," said Assistant Principal Snout.

"You've broken the NFA rule," screamed Ulna Mandible. *"I'm going to sue!"*

"You're going to pay for not inviting me to your parties," threatened Barton Slugg.

"I can't believe you almost got me to eat *his* toe cheese!" Fibby cried, pointing at Barton.

The Tardy Boys and their friends glanced sadly at one another. Their shoulders slumped in defeat. This was really, truly, the end.

"I instruct you to open that locker immediately," ordered Assistant Principal Snout.

Daisy glanced at Wade, who sadly nodded. There was no way to escape this time. They'd finally been caught. Daisy opened her locker. Inside lay a small, smelly, wrinkled, hairless, pink creature with a round head and a little round tummy. It almost looked like a little old naked bald man.

"You see!" Ulna Mandible shrieked. "I knew all along that they were hiding an animal!"

"But —" began Assistant Principal Snout.

"They've been doing it all day long!" Ulna Mandible screamed. "They've been lying and deceiving and breaking the rules!"

"Well, not —" Assistant Principal Snout tried to say.

"They ruined my daughter's model of the White House that cost me nearly five hundred dollars!" Ulna screeched, then pointed at Barton Slugg. "And they tried to get her to eat his disgusting toe cheese!"

"Hey!" Barton pouted. "My toe cheese isn't so bad. Besides, she was eating her own toe cheese long before she thought about eating mine."

Ulna ignored him and pointed at the Tardy Boys and their friends. "I demand you expel them from school permanently!"

"I can't," said Assistant Principal Snout.

"*What?!*" shouted Ulna Mandible. "*You will or I'll sue!*"

"But on what grounds would I expel them?" asked Assistant Principal Snout.

"*I just told you all the awful things they did,*" shrieked Ulna Mandible. "*And all of that is in addition to breaking the NFA rule!*"

"But they haven't broken the NFA rule," said Assistant Principal Snout.

"*Are you stupid and blind?!*" Ulna Mandible shrieked and pointed at Wheezy, nestled comfortably in the bottom of Daisy's locker. "*What do you think that is?*"

"It looks to me like a little bald, hairless, furless dog," said Assistant Principal Snout. "And being furless, it cannot break the No Furry Animals rule."

(GETTING CLOSER TO) THE END

Ulna Mandible's face turned bright red. *"What are you saying?"* she screamed.

"I'm saying I cannot punish students for breaking a rule they have not broken," said Assistant Principal Snout.

"Well, I've never!" Ulna Mandible shrieked. *"The nerve!"* She grabbed her daughter's hand. *"You are coming with me, Fibby! We are leaving this school forever!"*

Ulna started to drag Fibby down the hall. Suddenly, Principal Stratemeyer got on the public address system: "*Attention all teachers, staff, and students. We are receiving reports that the terrible odor has returned to the halls. Therefore, I have decided to close school early in order to conduct a thorough investigation of this matter. Please leave the building at once!*"

In an instant all the doors in the hallway opened and students and teachers poured out. The Tardy Boys and their friends were swallowed up in a sea of students rushing to get out of the building. Daisy got spun around. Leyton was shoved into a locker and Al-Ian was knocked off his feet and almost trampled. Wade thought he saw something small, pink, and bald go flying into the air, but he wasn't sure.

A few moments later, the hall was once again empty except for the Tardy Boys, their friends, and Assistant Principal Snout. Dazed by the onrush, the Tardy Boys and their friends struggled back to their feet. Assistant Principal Snout straightened his breathing mask. Daisy looked into her locker.

"Oh, no!" she cried. "Wheezy is gone!"

"And so is Barton!" said Al-Ian.

(SO CLOSE TO) THE END (THAT YOU CAN PROBABLY SMELL IT)

The Tardy Boys and their friends ran outside. Groups of kids were hurrying from the school as fast as they could.

"Now that Barton has left school grounds with Wheezy, he could go anywhere!" realized Leyton.

"And do anything he wants to with Wheezy!" added Al-Ian.

"He could nail Wheezy to a tree," said
Leyton.

"He could drop Wheezy in the sea,"
said Al-Ian.

"He could throw Wheezy in a lake,"
said Leyton.

"He could feed Wheezy to a snake,"
said Al-Ian.

Daisy turned pale and looked like she
was going to cry.

"Guys!" Wade shouted. "We have to
figure out where Barton went!"

"That's easy," said Al-Ian. "All we have
to do is follow his trail of slime."

Sure enough, a glistening trail of slime
led away from school. The Tardy Boys
and their friends started to follow it.

Suddenly Leyton pointed and shouted.
"There he is!"

Down the street stood a huge, muscular

man. His arms were as thick as car tires and his legs were as round as tree trunks. He had scars on his jaw and forehead, permanently swollen eyes, and a bent, crooked nose that looked like it had been broken at least twenty times. He was wearing black nylon shorts and a hooded black sweatshirt and looked like a professional wrestler, which is exactly what he was. In one of his muscular arms he cradled Wheezy. With his other arm he held a slimeball named Barton.

"Lemme go!" Barton cried, but the muscular man lifted him off the ground by his collar. Barton hung in the air swinging his arms and kicking his legs like a fish out of water.

"Mr. Roy!" Daisy ran toward him. "How did you find Barton?"

"I was coming to school to get Wheezy

and this boy ran toward me leaving a trail of slime and carrying my dog," answered Mr. Roy in a voice so deep that the branches of the trees shook when he spoke. "I could tell by the trail of slime that he was not the kind of boy who should have Wheezy."

"Lemme go!" Barton cried again and swung his arms and kicked his legs in the air.

"I'm so sorry, Mr. Roy," Daisy apologized. "Barton took Wheezy during a big commotion at school. We were just looking for him ourselves. And I'm also sorry that Wheezy lost all his fur."

"That's not your fault," said Mr. Roy.

"It's not?" gasped Daisy.

"No, it's my fault," said Mr. Roy. "I was in such a rush this morning that I forgot to give you Wheezy's zinc pills. If Wheezy doesn't take a pill every hour and a half, he starts to lose his fur."

"But we thought he was supposed to eat French cheese every hour and a half," said Wade.

"Yes, because the only way I can get him to take his pills is by hiding them in pieces of Camembert," Mr. Roy explained. "And don't worry, as soon as Wheezy gets his zinc pills again, his fur will grow right back."

"Lemme go!" Barton swung his arms and kicked his legs in the air, but didn't go anywhere.

"Anyway, I really want to thank you for taking care of Wheezy on such short notice," said Mr. Roy. "And as a reward, I have four front-row tickets for tomorrow night's Mega Wrestle Insanity Show at the Civic Center."

"I've always wanted to see that!" Leyton cried excitedly.

"Well, now you can." Mr. Roy smiled. He would have had a nice smile if he had not been missing so many teeth.

"Do aliens ever wrestle?" Al-Ian asked eagerly.

"Some of the guys sure do look like aliens," said Mr. Roy.

"Way cool!" cried Al-Ian.

"What about me?" asked Barton. "I never get invited to anything because everybody hates me. Can't I come, too?"

"Yes, you can," said Mr. Roy.

"Really!? Awesome!" cried Barton. "And can I have a front row seat, too?"

"Actually, Barton, you get to sit even closer," said Mr. Roy.

Barton gave the Tardy Boys and their friends a nasty and superior grin. "Nah-nah-na-na-nah! I get closer than you do!"

"That's right," said Mr. Roy. "You'll be right there in the wrestling ring with me."

(SO MUCH CLOSER TO) **THE END** (THAT YOU PROBABLY CAN'T STAND IT ANYMORE!)

That night when Daisy's parents got home from work they put on their tie-dyed clothes and threw an awesome party. All of Daisy's and the Tardy Boys' friends came. TJ came and wanted to know what happened with Wheezy at school that day.

Wade and Leyton told him how they managed to hide Wheezy in Daisy's locker the whole day and how Leyton and Al-Ian defeated Barton and Fibby in the great French Cheese versus Toe Cheese Debate.

"And we won because I had a good idea!" Leyton announced proudly.

"You?" TJ asked in amazement.

Wade patted his brother on the back. "I am proud of you, Leyton. You proved once and for all that if we drilled a tiny orifice into your skull and looked inside, we'd see something."

Leyton beamed with pride.

"And what happened to Fibby and Barton?" TJ asked.

"Fibby's mom took her out of school forever," said Wade. "And Barton has to wrestle Mr. Roy at the Mega Wrestle Insanity Show tomorrow night."

"So everything ended well," said Daisy.

"Except for one thing," TJ said with a frown. "What if my toilet trees don't grow by next summer? What will I bring to camp?"

Al-Ian frowned. "TJ, toiletries are things people use for personal grooming. Like toothbrushes, combs, and soap. If you go to sleepaway camp, you will probably be asked to bring toiletries. But you do not have to use them."

TJ smiled broadly. "Great!"

The doorbell rang. Daisy's parents didn't hear it because they were listening to peace-and-love music on their iPods so Daisy asked TJ to see who it was. A little while later TJ came back with a letter in his hand.

"Who was it?" Wade asked.

"An alien, I think," said TJ.

Al-Ian looked up, startled. "How do you know?"

"Well, it was green and had big bulging round eyes on either side of its head and four skinny legs and instead of hands it had long clawlike things," TJ said.

"A Mantis Alien!" Al-Ian gasped.

"It gave me this." TJ handed the letter to Wade. It was addressed to:

Wade, Leyton, and TJ Tardy
Planet Earth
Milky Way Galaxy

Wade tore it open and read:

Dear Sons,
You have probably been wondering what happened to your father and me and why you

have not heard from us in such a long time. The reason is that we were kidnapped by aliens. But don't worry. They are treating us nicely and promise to return us to Earth some-day. In the meantime, we hope you are eating well, and getting enough sleep and getting good grades in school. Don't forget to feed the cat.

Love,
Mom and Dad

Wade put down the letter and looked stunned. "That's amazing!"

"Unbelievable!" gasped TJ.

"Incredible!" agreed Daisy.

"I'll say," said Leyton. "I didn't know we had a cat!"

A POSTSCRIPT

Dear Reader,

Congratulations! You have just finished—or skipped to the end—of the first book in the brand-spanking-new Tardy Boys series. Of course, it isn't much of a series if there's only one book. But the author promises that there will soon be another book. And then the series will be two books long, making it THE SHORTEST SERIES EVER. This is because you really can't have a one-book series. Can you? I mean, if you could have one-book series, then EVERY BOOK would be a one-book series. And then what would stop anyone who has not written a book from claiming they wrote a NO-BOOK SERIES? And the next thing you know, not writing books will become another silly event in the Spring Olympics like rhythm gymnastics (dancing around with long ribbons), broom pushing, and chain-saw juggling.

Anyway, the title of the second book will be *Is That a Sick Cat in Your Backpack?* It will probably star the Tardy Boys since this is their series and it would be pretty strange to have a book in their series without them in it. There's a good chance Al-Ian and Daisy will be in it, too. Barton Slugg may make an appearance, but only if he can do something about his toe cheese. Assistant Principal Snout may show up if the author promises him that the furry animals involved will be wearing furry undergarments.

Any rumors you've heard about Alien Space Cats attacking the Earth in the next book are absolutely false. There is no such thing as Alien Space Cat Mind Control, either. The inhabitants of the Planet Meow in the Feline Galaxy are a friendly race. The Meowians are not planning to take over the Planet Earth and enslave all humans. The author of this book knows this is true because a Meowian stared deeply into his eyes and told him so.

Sincerely,
The Author